CHURCH BOY
IN THE DARK

A Dramatic Short Story about a Man,
the Love of God, and Sexuality

To Barb & Norm,
It has been and will continue to be a blessing having the both of you as new friends forever. Thank You For Being The Best
Much Love & Respect

HAR'RELL

[signature]

PAGE PUBLISHING, INC.
New York, NY

First originally published by Page Publishing, Inc. 2017

ISBN 978-1-68409-774-6 (Paperback)
ISBN 978-1-68409-775-3 (Digital)

Printed in the United States of America

Foreword

When "Kevin," as I affectionately know him, first told me that he was writing a book, I asked him if it would be okay for me to write the foreword for the book. He said that he would like that; "It would be an honor." Now I don't know if he agreed because I am his younger sister or simply because he felt that I had the ability to do it. Whatever the reason, I am also honored to have been given the opportunity. As children you argue, fight, disagree, make up, and then start the process all over again, but never do you expect to experience the path that life takes you on as individuals.

Who are we to judge one another? We are put on this earth to learn life's lessons and then share those lessons with the next generation. We all take different paths and make choices that may not be pleasing to our fellow human beings but they're our choices to make. I am not a member of a church but a member of the Kingdom and the human race, and I've learned a lot about us. We preach about what Jesus Christ, Allah, Jehovah, the Buddha, and Waheguru, to name a few, say, who instruct us to do what is pleasing to Him, but do we always do it?

Of course not. If we did, the world would not function as it does and we would not have to discover, through his eyes, what Har'rell discusses in this book. No matter what religion, as true believers, we should all be able to respect one another and not judge. All the things that we are doing now have already been discussed in the Bible, Quaran, Dhammapada, and the Adi Granth (a.k.a. Guru Granth Sahib). We continue to teach from these writings, but rarely do we listen or adhere to what is being taught. I am not saying I am judging the human race but merely observing and giving my observation.

As you read this book, open your mind, body, and spirit. Remove all judgment not to judge but to think clearly, and when you do, I guarantee you, you will see yourself in this book. Think of all the things you have done, the people you've met and turned away from, and then ask yourself, "Am I really pleasing myself, my fellow beings, and most of all, my prophet or God?"

Natarsia L. Joye, MPA

I dedicate this book first to God and to my Lord and Savior Jesus Christ for revelation. His testimony of life and death has been my inspiration from the first Bible story I ever heard "The Virgin Mary." All that I am and all that I will become is because of His sacrifice, His Life for ours.

Secondly, to the angels who have encamped themselves around me. Their heavenly spirits protect me and guide me on the course this journey called destiny. "Grandmama" Eartha Lee Chisolm, "Grandaddy" Henry Chisolm, "Gramps" Arthur and Rosa Herbert Sr., Uncle Lloyd, Aunt Joan, Aunt Celestine Boston–Tolbert, Uncle Pin, my brothers Police Officer William L. Chisolm and Anthony Herbert, Steven Arce, Michael Winfield (my best friend), Kenneth "Kenny" Gatch, and those who have recently gone on but are still connected.

Count it not strange when a spirit, an angel, comes to visit upon you; God uses them to protect you. They are connected to your energy and you to theirs even in death.

To my mother, Mrs. Celestine Chisolm-Herbert, and stepfather, Arthur Herbert, thank you for being wonderful role models for us children. Although you had to sacrifice two of us and give them back to God, you never faltered in your love and strength to me and my sister Natarsia. Our success stems directly from your support and encouragement to strive to be our best selves; I adore both of you. My sister, Natarsia, you are and have always been the female friend any man coming of age needs in his life. Thanks for keeping it real. I know we have had our tough times with one another, especially through relationships, but had it not been for you, I don't think I could have ever understood how to actually accept and nurture my relationships with men or women. My cousin Abdul affectionately known to me us as "Jimmy," whose unique expression can be heard in his literary piece entitled <u>"An Ugly Man's Journey"</u>, thank you for always seeing God in me in despite of my shortcomings. Your words inspire and inform. "Ray Brown," hair-cutting genius, thank you. Steven Tribble, you guided me during the toughest times I had in Indianapolis and were a great support not only during the custody battle of me obtaining my son but in raising him as well. You were definitely another parent in his life during his darkest hour; much love and respect to you.

Bishop Eddie Long, thank you for years of supernatural teachings and a word to my vision that has me still moving forward today. Pastor Craig L. Oliver of Elizabeth Baptist Church (my present pastor), it is your boldness and realness that has allowed me to now be bold and come forward with this vision book.

In my early teens to young adult years, God placed me around great young men of God. When I met them and spent years in their presence, they were directors, song writers, and musicians of the Bronx Mass Choir, Mt. Vernon Community Choir, and Love Fellowship Crusade Choir . . .

thank you, Pastor Kervy Brown, Pastor Roger Hambrick, Bishop Eric McDaniel, Bishop Hezekiah Walker, and Bishop Brian D. Moore for instilling in me the tools for carrying the boldness of God's presence in my life early in life.

What I am is because of how God made me. Who I am is because of what you taught me of being a man of God first and everything else after will make me the gentleman. You may not totally agree with everything in this this book and may even want to confront me on some of these things. I still have to say thank you.

Special thanks to Damon Flanagan Tahziyah for your incredible graphic and artist talents throughout the years. You have been the vehicle that created the image I have today and this book cover, and Anare V. Holmes for presenting me in the media in Indianapolis, Indiana, and following my events as they formed, also for you expert editing of this manuscript. God bless both of you. It is no happenstance that God has placed both of you right here in Atlanta with me all the way from Indianapolis. Our work is just beginning.

INTRODUCTION

I am from generations of clergymen; my fourth great-grandfather was a clergyman and so was his son. My biological father was a pastor of a church in Columbia, South Carolina, until his death. Today my family has male and female ministers who are also professionals in the workforce. I always knew I had a calling, but it just seemed to be a calling of a different kind.

On December 25, 1967, Christmas Day in Charleston, South Carolina, a vessel was born to Celestine Chisolm. She named this child **Har'rell Kevin Cavon Chisolm**. As she was a single mother of now two boys at only twenty years old, God told her to move. But she could only take one son. So when Har'rell turned eight months old, Celestine packed her things and, with very little money, moved herself and this brand-new baby to New York City, a small-city Southern girl with this vessel, a gift to an enormous revelation of God, in her arms. From the time the baby could walk, he was speaking with boldness! Today I am a forty-plus-year-old single parent who happened to have been born homosexual. I don't doubt my birth because I don't doubt the vision that God has placed on my life in spite of what the world feels about those like me. As many children who are born imperfect, we have battled and questioned for years, "Why, God, were we born this way" We endure persecuting directives to scriptures in the bible that says God hates who we are, although you also say that God knew who we were before we came here. I wrote the dramatic short story leg of this book in the course of the six weeks of the twelve weeks that I was lying in bed, waiting to die. In the first six weeks, I received calls from family saying their goodbyes. My parents were requesting my funeral and burial wishes. My son and partner were trying to manage one another's life without me.

It has been a struggle for me as to why this was so, and then I thought about Adam and Eve, not in the humiliating sense that straight folks delve into against us. How Eve, a disobedient straight woman, caused all women to have imperfect births, that not only would she have to endure pain during childbirth but she bled and cramped monthly before having the ability to conceive. She could have a child with no arms, no legs, one who was mentally disabled, autistic, blind, mute, deaf, with too many male chromosomes, or too many female chromosomes. I questioned even why I was so masculine, but then I had to understand the levels of chromosomes that would take a male or female to feeling so much more of the opposite gender that they would seek to change their gender. I have my personal views about that

7

and my spiritual views within this book. I was raised by a stepfather who was a New York City police officer and a mom who was a nurse. I attended private school and had a very positive upbringing, sang with gospel choirs and in nightclubs, ran track, worked with mentally retarded children, and more. However, the reality is, as strict as my parents were, I still learned quickly that having another life behind closed doors that no one else knows about but you and those you were doing it with may not be seen by everyone exactly, not what you're doing in the dark, but actually, your state of mind, physical, and financial condition will scream "Dysfunction!" And God will expose you in the light among others.

I am proud to say that I raised not just a son but also a good man. He is intelligent, well-mannered, respectful, and yes, he is ready to be a good father and an even better husband. Many say that homosexuals cannot raise healthy straight children, as though there is some sort of rub-off factor. Those of us who have children raise our children based on the same values, if not better, than those we received from our parents. Now isn't that a surprise! Because of my parents' teachings and supportive ways, I was able to stand by my son to the point of him going from being a very misbehaved student and gang member to a young man who began Le Cordon Bleu College Culinary Arts at age sixteen, went into the military in 2008 at age seventeen, and by age nineteen, he is now in the Army not only as a cook but also a Ranger/Airborne. In 2009, he served in Afghanistan, and through my prayers and that of others, he saw death but not his own.

So I pray that this book brings us together as a people as we learn more of one another and embrace the differences that we have created and those that God created. I wrote this book for you, the straight male and female, because I love all people, and had it not been for you, gay or lesbian people would not exist. But sometimes we hate what we don't understand because it is easier to do that and form an opinion than to gain facts from gaining knowledge.

I could talk about what you're about to read and prepare you for what may open up emotions held deep within inside those places not yet explored in yourself, but I won't. We are not held accountable for the things we do not know. Even the Bible tells us we perish because of lack of knowledge, but lack of knowledge can be dangerous for our children and grandchildren if we do not make ourselves aware of what's out there. There are predators lurking and seeing our children every day. The predators smile and wave good morning to us and, at the same time, draw themselves close to our precious gifts. What then do you say to the child with the scars our children may carry way into adulthood, when more guidance, supervision and communication would have prevented some of their life-changing experiences?

It is time to reeducate our youth about our current world and reveal why they must commit to education and less media influence. Reality shows, news broadcasts, and videos are a quick fix to our life situations and do not give our youth a true perspective on real life. Many children and some adults model and emulate characters they see on television, whether it is violence or sex or behaviors good and bad. What they fail to realize is that when the thirty minutes are over, so is that show.

Life is not a performance. Just ask the storyteller of this book, Samuel. Samuel was an eighties teen and what he witnessed growing up in the city of New York back then can only be told through his eyes and in his own words. He also invited a few of his friends, whom you will also meet in this book. They have much to share with you, and maybe, just maybe, they are you.I hope you will enjoy the journey through life in Samuel's world. He is a great person, with a wealth of information, who met God, the church, and the New York City streets early and almost never let it go until . . . well, I will let you begin. Long introductions wouldn't do this book any justice, so I'll just leave you with . . . *Church Boy in the* Dark and *Inside of Insight Magazine*!

MY TESTIMONY

Earvin "Magic" Johnson retired abruptly in 1991 after announcing that he had HIV but returned to play in the 1992 All-Star Game, winning the All-Star MVP Award. After protests from his fellow players, he retired again for four years but returned in 1996 to play **thirty-two** games for the Lakers before retiring for the third and final time. He is to this day an advocate and spokesperson for HIV/AIDS**,** among many other noted celebrities. Unfortunately**,** their message has gone on without an understanding of its significance in him coming forward to the public. He wanted us to know that no matter how famous or how rich you are**,** you too can be infected. Instead we revere him for his courage and wonderful things he has done for the business industry but still look down on others who **do** not **have** celebrity status.

In 1991, I was diagnosed with the HIV virus. I was devastated that at age twenty-three I was going to die, which back then is what we were told. Prior to this date, I had several friends who had died from the disease AIDS even someone I was dating in 1987 had died from AIDS. However, years seemed to go by, and I was still fine and not having any complications. So I went on with my life. In 2000, I gained full custody of my only child. I thought that it would not be a challenge, but unfortunately, while living in Indianapolis, Indiana, during one of their worst winters, I contracted pneumonia, which inflamed my AIDS condition.

My viral load was over 181,000. I had gained opportunistic infections that also did not have cures. I lost thirty pounds and became bedridden for weeks. I was dying; each day I became worse than the day before. I did not want to die in the hospital, so I remained at home. It's funny what you become well in your spirit with when death is near. My partner at the time became the surrogate parent for my son. When he had appointments or if I had to show up at the school, he went in my place. We were afraid that if anyone found out that I was in the house dying, they would take my son away from me. I had no family in Indianapolis other than him and his estranged mother and sister. By the sixth week, I began to call family, and they began to call me to say our good-byes. My mom and I made my funeral plans, and I accepted that I was about to die. Somehow after all those calls were made, over the next few days, God spoke to me and said I needed to tell my story. I could barely sit up right. But in the middle of the night, each week as I wrote a chapter of the dramatic short story, I began to gain strength! I could barely see out of my right eye—I felt I was going blind—but with one eye open and my body weak and feeble, I pressed on. Every day, my son would come home from school, peep in my room, and say, "Dad, Dad?" just to ensure I was alive. This one day in particular, he came in, and I was up vacuuming the living room. I had begun dinner, and I was singing God's praises throughout the house. I decided to find an infectious disease doctor. I asked him if he thought I was going to make it, and he said, "Yes, if you have faith." Well, I had that and then some. Now as the book came to a close, I realized that I was not dying, so I could not end it with my death. At age forty-two, I am still here and have allowed God to use me as His vessel to do whatever He calls me to do. I have a business that is in the business of restoring and developing entrepreneurs. The final three sections of this book God revealed to me this year. I pray that by God using me as an example, more people will come forward and get tested, treated, or preventive education on HIV/AIDS. I have had two partners who were HIV negative when we met, and they are HIV negative today. We had full intimacy, but I protected their life; that's being mature. Now they know to protect others. Unprotected sex, for thirty minutes of pleasure, is not worth years of medicine, health deterioration, anger, and death. Hating and hurting each other leads to death also . . . death of one's spirit.

Pall Bearers

THE 1ST BAT,75TH RANGER REGIMENT
HUNTER ARMY AIRFIELD OF
SAVANNAH, GEORGIA

Honorary Pall Bearers

Terrell Simmons   Tareeq Abdul-Malik

James Robinson   Radwan Abdul-Malik

Lawrence Chisolm   Illilyin Abdul-Malik

Abdur Rahman Farrakhan   Ronnie Robinson Jr.

Tajjuddin Abdul-Hakim   Major Clay Middleton

Joseph Herbert & Antonio & Yaphet Bienvenue

In Appreciation

On behalf of the entire family of SSgt. Chisolm, we wish to express our deep appreciation to all brothers and sisters in Christ who have stood with us during this time of bereavement. We indeed appreciate your personal visits, prayers, and more especially to all those who took out their precious time to celebrate Avonye' (John)' transition into God' Kingdom

The Almighty God reward your kindness with greater measure.

And to all our guests and **Special Battalion Hunter Army Airfield & Staff**, may the Good Lord bless you and grant you journey mercies back to your respective homes in Jesus Name. Amen. Thank you all so much.

–The Chisolm, Anderson and Herbert Family

Funeral Services Entrusted to:

Palmetto Mortuary
1122 Morrison Drive
Charleston, SC 29403
Phone (843)727-1230

In Honor of your Memory

AVONYE' JOHN CAVON CHISOLM

August 1, 1990 - August 26, 2016

Bethany Baptist Church
790 Meeting Street Charleston, SC 29403
Rev. Dr. Eric L Mack, Officiating

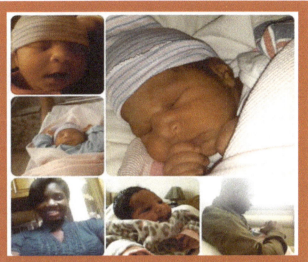

Scripture Selections

I lift up my eyes to the mountains—
where does my help come from?
My help comes from the Lord,
the Maker of heaven and earth.
He will not let your foot slip—
he who watches over you will not slumber;
indeed, he who watches over Israel
will neither slumber nor sleep.
The Lord watches over you—
the Lord is your shade at your right hand;
the sun will not harm you by day,
nor the moon by night.
The Lord will keep you from all harm—
he will watch over your life;
the Lord will watch over your coming and going
both now and forevermore.
(Psalm 121: 1-8)

"Do not let your hearts be troubled.
You believe in God; believe also in me.
My Father's house has many rooms;
if that were not so,
would I have told you that I am going there to prepare a place for you?
And if I go and prepare a place for you,
I will come back and take you to be with me that you also may be where I am.
You know the way to the place where I am going."

Thomas said to him, "Lord, we don't know where you are going,
so how can we know the way?"
Jesus answered, "I am the way and the truth and the life.
No one comes to the Father except through me.
(John 14:1-6)

Obituary for Avonye' John Cavon Chisolm

Staff Sergeant Avonye' J.C. Chisolm of Hunter Army Airfield entered Eternal Rest on August 26th, 2016 at Memorial Hospital In Savannah, Georgia. He was the Son of Mr. Har'rell Chisolm PA,PLL of Atlanta, GA and The Late Ms. Monique Anderson of Goldsboro, NC. One daughter Aaliyah Burgess proceeded him in death. The Brother of Mrs. Jeannette (Deontae) Anderson of Goldsboro, NC. The Grandson of Arthur (Jay) & Celestine Herbert of North Charleston, SC and the late John and Jeannette Anderson and the late Rev. Kenneth Cash and great grandson of Claretta Cash and the late Leon (Lucky) of Charleston, SC and great-great grandson of the late Henry and Earthalee Chisolm. The nephew of Natarsia (Andrew) Joye-Lawrence and Patricia Smith of Bronx, NY. Simone Moore of Syracuse, NY, Giselle Washington of Sandford, NC, Audrinne Tyson of Greenville, NC, grand aunts include Mary L Simmons of Charleston, SC, Blondell (Ronnie) Robinson of Winston Salem of NC, Leola Cash, Naomi (late Louis) Collins, Cathy Cash of Charleston, SC, Verbena (Charles) Brown of Hilton Head, SC. Two aunts Joan Chisolm and Lili. Five uncles Police officer William Chisolm, Anthony Herbert, Lloyd Chisolm, Leon Cash Jr. and Reginald Cash proceeded him in death. Two God-fathers Austin Holmes and Rashad Carson of Atlanta, GA.

The funeral service for Staff Sgt. Chisolm will be held on Wednesday, August 31, 2016 at 12 noon at Bethany Baptist Church 790 Meeting Street Charleston, SC 29403 delivered by Rev. Dr. Eric L Mack, Pastor.

Wake service will be held from 6-8pm at Bethany Baptist Church 790 Meeting Street Charleston, SC 29403 and family will be receiving friends and family.

God Made Us a Family

Order of Service

Minister Officiating:	**Rev. Dr. Eric L Mack, Pastor**
	Bethany Baptist Church
Processional	*"I Give Myself Away"*
	Bethany Choir
Prayer:	**Natarsia Joy-Lawrence**
Scripture Reading:	
Old Testament: Psalms 121: 1-2	**Natarsia Joy-Lawrence**
New Testament: John 14:1-6	**Jeannette Anderson**
Ushering in of The Holy Spirit	*"When The Saints Go to Worship"*
	Har'rell K.C. Chisolm & Kenya Simmons (Cousin)
Special Tribute (2 mins)	**Sgt. Josh Henderson** of
	1st Bat 75th Ranger Regiment
	SPC Devon Parrish of
	Fort Benning, SC
Hymn Preparation	**Bethany Choir**
Words of Comfort	**Elder Israiel M Brodrick**
Committal	**Rev. Dr. Eric L Mack, Pastor**
Benediction	**Rev. Dr. Eric L Mack, Pastor**

Recessional   Avonye' Favorite Song   **Jeannette Anderson**   " Open Up My Heart"

Repast at Bethany Baptist Church immediately after services.

Interment
Sunset Memorial Gardens
2915 Ashley Phosphate Rd
North Charleston, SC 29418

Depicted from the Book

CHURCH BOY
IN THE DARK

And From the Dramatic Soap Opera Stage Play *"From rhe Pulpit, To the Pews"*

Comes the Highly Anticipated Movie:

HEAVY
IS THE HEAD THAT WEARS THE
CROWN

ELOHIM PRODUCTIONS, Inc

PRESENTED BY: ELOHIM PRODUCTIONS INC.

SPONSORED BY: XPOSURE IMAGE GROUP & EYES ENTERTAINMENT

DEBUTING SUMMER 2018

XPOSURE

EYES
ENTERTAINMENT INC.

From The Dramatic Short Story of

CHURCH BOY
IN THE DARK

Comes the Dramatic Soap Opera Stage Play:

FROM THE
PULPIT
TO THE
PEWS

PRESENTED BY: ELOHIM PRODUCTIONS INC.
SPONSORED BY: XPOSURE IMAGE GROUP & EYES ENTERTAINMENT

ATLANTA, GA THANKSGIVING WEEKEND 2017

HONOR

❧ AVONYE' JOHN CAVON CHISOLM ❧

AUGUST 1, 1990 – AUGUST 26, 2016

we honor your life and sacrafice...love dad

GRANDPA TAKE ME TO CHURCH

THE FIRST CHAPTER

Momma was sweet "Georgia Brown" in the flesh. Her smooth copper skin, baked from her heritage that stemmed from the coast of the West Indies to the Isles of Psalm of South Carolina. I swore that Coca-Cola must have designed its bottles after her figure; at least that's what the men would say when we walked by. Momma was different from other women and yet very much the same. Because although she set out for the big city of New York for a better life, love in all the wrong places seemed to travel right along with us. However, that did not stop her from pursuing her dreams of becoming a doctor. As I said, she was different. By age twenty-six, she had already given birth to all five of us children: Natalie, Kenneth, Winston, Carina, and me, Samuel. I'm the youngest. In many ways, I was like an only child, because every time you saw Momma, you saw me. She always told me that I was her precious jewel and that she felt that out of the five of us, I needed more protection.

I figured she said that because I was so little and born on Christmas. We were stair- step-children, so we were all close in age. The oldest, Natalie, was twelve. She was already built like a woman and acted like one too. Dang, she got on my nerves. When Momma went to school, she left the warden in charge; it's no wonder she became a lawyer. She could tell a story of lies so well no judge or jury could save us if she wanted to convict us of pissing her off. I gave her the most trouble on purpose. Most of the time, Momma would have to send me to someone else to be looked after while she was gone because Natalie refused to watch me. That was cool with me. I was five with a mind of a nine-year-old and just as adventurous. Being around Natalie left me no room to roam. This one day in particular, Momma said she was going shopping for our school clothes. She hardly ever took us with her to shop. Imagine five kids in all that busy city confusion. However, she did take me along on that day. We got on the bus, and off we went. As I looked around the bus, I noticed a sea of eyes just gaping at my momma and me. So I just stared back, waiting for someone to say why he or she was in our grill. Then a female, about my momma's age or younger, said to her, "So how old is he?"

Momma, with a little sass in her voice, said, "The child is five." The lady replied, "He's gonna be one fine-ass black man when he gets older." Then chimed in this guy sitting next to her, "Oh yes, a real heartbreaker, with his big pretty eyes and bright pink lips! Girl, you cruising little boys now, miss thing? Aren't there enough fine men in New York for you? What, you gotta go to Romper Room? Oh hell no, you did not, Ms. Toto, you are no Dorothy, so allow me to click three heels and whirlwind you back to Kansas, honey! You don't want it! I will spill all your dirt! What about them boys from Taft High School with your twenty-four-year-old a-mmmmm! Girl, you almost made me cuss in front of this child!" He then looked over at my momma and said, "I am sorry, sistah, but I mean no disrespect here to you or him. I just feel he is so precious. Now back to you, hepher! Girl, you sit in your car and wait outside of that school for the catch of the day, as though the fish market decided to switch to beef! And you know what I am talking about, Miss Daddy, don't come for me—you know I know what you really like on occasion, honey!" Momma looked down at me; I looked up at her. We smiled, then she kissed me on my forehead, looked up at those two individuals with a long, disgusted stare on her face, and then held me closer to her. By now, I already knew what that look meant. It meant that the person or persons had said too much around me, something they most definitely should not have said. So I kept looking at the two individuals who just caused the whole bus to stare at me with my own look of disgust, and I did not even know why. I felt the need to be loyal to my mom. I was even ready to defend her if I had to. In the South Bronx, you learn early how to defend yourself. As the bus ride continued, the male seemed to never stop looking at me, even when everyone else had long stopped paying attention to me. It appeared he was waiting for me to say something. So I did. I said, "What do you want? My momma already got a boyfriend." He laughed and proclaimed, "Yeah, child, and so do I." The laughter erupted throughout the bus. I did not understand what that meant, at least not then. My momma did not seem to think it was very funny. We came to our stop, and as we were getting off the bus, the dynamic duo both said, "Bye, Samuel!" I looked back at them hard and fast, puzzled by what I just heard, and asked, "How do you know my name?" I asked. The guy said, "It's on your shirt, you forgot." I said, "Ooooooh, bye!" I never wore that shirt again.

I loved Sundays. Momma would get up early, fix breakfast, and start dinner for later, all at the same time. Natalie would call herself getting us ready for church. I always had to show her how to make my clothing look nice. After breakfast, we would go out to the street, Momma would hail a cab, and we would pile in. We would be dressed to the nines. I just knew we were the richest kids in the South Bronx. We always had nice things although we did live in the projects. "Start small, have it all," Momma would always say. In the '70s, the projects were not so bad, just crowded as hell. Our church was in Harlem on 125th Street. I loved Harlem. It just seemed so alive to me. At the time, that was the furthest I had ever been in Manhattan. The Empire State Building seemed like it was in another city to me because I only saw it on television or from the highway at a long distance. Our church was nice but kind of small. Momma said most of the people there were from her hometown in South Carolina. They all had those accents that sounded like they were singing even when they were not. Momma was an usher and would sit us down in our seats before moving to her post. Ushers looked more like bodyguards to me at that time. They were always telling people what to do and what not to do. The pastor of the church was tall, dark, and obviously good-looking, and believe it or not, at age six, I noticed how attractive he was. His skin was very dark but smooth, his teeth were white, and when he smiled, it made you smile. I would be glued to his every word. He would lick his lips slowly; after each time, he took a sip of water. The church had many women but none quite as fine as Momma. He always seemed to acknowledge her while he preached. "God said in His Word we must be fruitful and multiply, ain't that right, Sis Carla?" Natalie would get angry when he acknowledged Momma in the middle of his sermons. She said he was making fun of Momma because she had so many kids and no husband.

But I noticed every time Momma would stand up front during offering time, he had his eyes fixed all on her backside as though a movie was showing during service. He had a look in his eye that I now know to be the look of lust, but I did not realize how dangerous the look could be and its manifestation. I remember one night Momma and I went to the church. She said the pastor wanted her to come in to assist him with some bookkeeping. When we got there, he shook my hand and asked me to go into the nursery to read some of the books or play with toys while he and the college girl, as he put it, got some work done. I sat for a while—I would say for at least forty-five minutes—then out slammed my momma running and crying and her clothes were all torn! "Come on, Sammy, hurry! We have to go now." Momma hailed a cab and we went straight to my uncle's house on the other side of town. We arrived at my uncle's house, and both he and my mom went into the other room. I could only hear part of what they were saying, but from what I could hear, there was going to be some trouble at the church. Suddenly my uncle stormed out of the room! He went into the closet near the door, pulled out a black small case, then left saying he would never try to rape another woman again! Not in this life anyway. All I know is we never went back to that church, and from my understanding, a few weeks later, neither did that pastor.

Over the course of the next month, church was never mentioned in our house on Sunday until I asked my mother one morning if we could go to church with the Taylors. They were our neighbors that lived directly below us. She said, "If you want to go, ask them if they will take you, but I am not going anywhere where I can't trust the man who is supposed to represent God and His Word." So I called the Taylors. Natalie, Winston, and I were the only three that wanted to go. Kenneth and Carina decided to stay home with Momma. I enjoyed going with them. We went consistently for about one year. Then all of a sudden, Natalie and Winston stopped wanting to go. By this time, I was now nearly eight years old and loved church so much that I did not care if they were not going I still wanted to go. I went to church with the Taylors for about two years thereafter. Then it just seemed as though I was missing something. This was not my family, and I felt strange every time people would comment on the Taylors and their well-mannered children. I was well mannered but not because of the Taylors; I wanted to be with my own family.

My grandparents eventually moved to New York as well, which was the highlight of my early life. I hardly ever saw them, except during Christmas when Momma would take us down south to visit. My grandparents were the epitome of sophistication with West Indian and African pride. Now I knew where my momma got her style of dress from and why she made sure we always looked well. She used to say, "When you walk out that door, you represent me." One evening, my grandpa was over for dinner, and he was talking about this church he had been going to. The pastor was an old friend of his from the early 1950s. My grandma— well, she boasted of a church in Harlem on 135th Street on the corner of Lenox Avenue. It was a nice church; I went with her every now and again, but my grandpa had a finesse that I wanted to own for myself one day. I saw that as opportunity knocking. I immediately asked Grandpa if he would take me to church with him. He seemed unsure at first, and then he looked me in my eyes and said, "Only if you behave and do not get into anything." He also was a deacon and did not have time to babysit me. I agreed to be good. So the following Sunday, off we went to his church in the North Bronx. I loved when Grandpa came to pick me up. He had the sweetest Cadillac Coupe De Ville. The women in the neighborhood used to swoon over him as he entered the building and seemed to wait for him to come back out. They would be lined in front of the building. My grandpa was a sharp dresser, as he was quite fond of his Brooks Brothers suits and stylish shoes. I loved the way people watched us as we got into his car. I just looked and waved as though we were a parade. Some days, though, my grandpa didn't want go straight home after church. Some days we went to Harlem so he could play his numbers and visit his buddies at Smalls Paradise. Then some days, we went over to Aunt Cecilia's house. Funny though, Grandpa always said to me, "Don't tell your Grandma or your mama we went to see your aunt. They don't care for her much." I never said a word because I loved my grandpa and I loved being around him. Cecilia was as light as any white woman I had ever seen, but I figured she was still black 'cause all the pictures of people in her house were her complexion or darker. Cecilia was pretty and younger than my grandma but older than my mom's oldest sister. I did not understand how she was my aunt. She was very nice to me. So I did not mind that she and Grandpa spent most of our visit alone together in her bedroom. I just waited because I knew that when we left, I could ask for almost anything and Grandpa would buy it for me. My grandpa was a good man; he just loved life in excess. Gambling, drinking, and women were his vices. Well, later, those three combined ended what most would call his days of destruction.

Grandpa was my church buddy for years until I became, I would say, about fourteen years old. It was at that age I met a girl, Michaunda, and that was all she wrote; my hormones were in full bloom. I wanted to be her boyfriend, but she only let me be her friend. Ha haaaa! But that changed some years later. You know a man can blossom through his teens. I began going to church with her and her family. I will get back to you about Michaunda and me later; we didn't stay buddies for long. I am grateful for the two years of friendship though before we found out what puppy love can bring into the world . . . or not bring. Well, I'll go into it later, life experiences; let's just say, "Came out of the woodwork around me." I would say, "Hold on to your seat," but you are probably sitting down already. I just wish someone knew half of the things that were happening to me so I could have had fewer skeletons in my closet.

Harlem World . . . in the World

The Second Chapter

It was now the summer of 1981; my momma was no longer a single woman or a med student. She was now Dr. Carla Richardson. And yes, her last name was no longer Lampier like us children. She met a supervisor of emergency medical technicians while on the job, and they married. I used to tease her about how funny she looked in her scrubs. I guess Mr. Raymond Richardson didn't think so. Even with five children, he loved and respected her so much that he could not let her get away. He wanted to adopt us and give us his last name, but my brothers mostly felt to be loyal to our grandfather and his name. Natalie and Kenneth had gone off to college. Winston—well, he just graduated high school and wanted to follow in Raymond's footsteps and become an EMT. Carina was going into her senior year, and I was now a junior in high school. We moved into a large home in the North Bronx. It was nice, but I still had the desire to be in Manhattan. My high school was also in the Bronx. Actually, it was in the South Bronx, only blocks away from the bridge that led into Harlem. In order to be closer to all the action, I convinced my mom to let me move in with my grandparents. They lived in walking distance from not only my high school but Yankee Stadium as well and, of course, another bridge that led into Harlem. I joined the basketball team as well as work four days a week after school in the evenings and weekends, which allowed me flexibility of time. Some evenings after practice, I did not get home until 6:30 p.m. My part time job in midtown Manhattan at Nathan's Famous Franks did not get me home until 11:00 p.m.

I had not yet known how much free time this type of schedule would allow me. As I said earlier, I was adventurous and wanted to be a part of everything. There was a group started in Harlem, sort of a citywide singing group. We sang gospel as well as inspirational music. We traveled all over New York. I did not realize how large this city was until I joined this group. The group had people from ages thirteen to fifty. You could only imagine the things I became exposed to, having had such a diverse group of people come into my life. There was this one gentleman—I guess someone told him that if you drink a shot of vodka before you sing, your voice would be clearer, because his breath smelled of it every rehearsal. Then there were the stars, those who sang so well they wanted you to know it. They sang loud and always adlibbed; even when we were silent, they had to sing a tune. It got on my nerves, so I did not stay with this group very long. I eventually joined up with a group of guys looking for another male vocalist to start a gospel group. I was a big fan of Commissioned and the Winans, so being with this group seemed more my speed. The addition of rehearsals and singing engagements to my schedule left me with nearly no time at home. For my sixteenth birthday, my mom gave me a big party, of course at a community center in the South Bronx because that's where most of my friends lived. I called this my prelude into adulthood. Unfortunately, this party was not the only thing that catapulted me into adulthood. One afternoon, it was a rare day for me. I would say by now it was May, five months after my sixteenth birthday. I had no basketball practice, I was off from work, and I had $80 in my pocket from my recent paycheck. I decided to go to a record store on 145th street to purchase some cassettes. Instead of going home to drop off my books—at the time, I was still living with my grandparents—I decided to just walk on over the 149th Street bridge into Harlem. How was I to know this would be the day that would change my entire life forever? As I walked across the bridge, I noticed a guy coming toward me. He was very muscular in his stature but not very tall, maybe 5'9", although he was taller than me. As he walked past me, I noticed he was staring directly in my face and did not blink once. I turned around as we passed each other to see if he was still looking, and he was. He stopped in the middle of the bridge and waved for me to come back. Curiosity was getting the best of me. I was a good swimmer, so if the East River was my next destination, I was prepared, and running was always the first option. So I walked over to where he was standing on the bridge. He introduced himself and without a second breath said to me, "Damn, boy, you've got the prettiest eyes." I did not know what to say to him. I wore glasses, so it did not make sense to me, and what was this tough-looking man doing talking to me like I was some female? His name was Vance. He said, "Most people would say thank you." "Thanks," I said and began to walk away. He trotted behind me and stopped me once again. "I didn't get your name, little man," he replied. "Samuel," I said. He said, "Well, Samuel, how long have you been going to Cardinal Hayes High School?" "How do you know if I'm even in high school?" I chuckled. He said, "The name is on your bag." You would have thought I learned my lesson eleven years ago, when I was five. I told him that I was a junior. That seemed to please him. He said, "Oh! You are older than I thought." He asked if I lived in Harlem. I said, "No, the Bronx, but I am on my way to the record store." He said that he was in a hurry but if I could get away later, he wanted to see me later. I asked what about. He said that he had other surprises as well, but not to worry, he would not do anything to hurt a cool young brother; he just thought I was interesting and wanted to learn more about me. He said just to hang out—you know, like a mentor and kick it. He asked if I played any sports. I said, "Yes, I am on the basketball team." He said, "Well, now you know what we will talk more about." He instructed me to take a taxi to 145th and Amsterdam Avenue at 6:30 p.m.; he would be outside waiting for me. I said okay and went on my way. I looked back one last time, and he looked back again, smiled, and went toward the Bronx. I went to the record store and purchased my records but immediately realized the time, and it was nearing the time that I would leave practice. I took the subway from the 145th in order to get to 161st Street and Yankee Stadium quick because I needed to give my grandmother the excuse I had to work and make it look as though I had just left basketball practice. I made it just in the nick of time, and as soon as I walked in the door, she said, "Boy, look at the time—don't you have to go to work?" "Are you going to be in by ten o'clock, the usual time? "No, I might stay a little later. I owe the manager one hour from her letting me off early last week. "Okay, be careful and do not forget to ride in the third car with the conductor!" she exclaimed. I said okay, grabbed my uniform, and left immediately. I hung out in a nearby arcade around the corner from Yankee Stadium until 6:15 p.m. I left there and hailed a taxi. As we approached the top of the hill of Amsterdam Avenue, there he was. I don't know why I thought he would not be there. I asked the driver how much, and before I could pay the driver, Vance pulled out a twenty and handed it to him. He asked if I was hungry. I said no, I had already eaten. I asked him if he lived around there; he said nearby. He said, "I have to stop in here." It was a motel on the corner. I took a deep breath and said to myself, *Well, Sammy, what have you gotten yourself into and what are you going to do to get yourself out?* I followed him in; strange, though, he had a key to one of the rooms. As we entered the room, I noticed that on the bed was a bag of grapes, clearly weed; I had smoked it once before so I was no stranger to it, and there was something else that I was a stranger to. It was white and looked like confectioner's sugar. I actually thought for a second that he must have been dipping his grapes into the sugar. He told me to have a seat on the bed, so I did. He offered me something to drink; he gave me juice in a tall glass. He rolled a joint and lit it up; I was very uncomfortable because for someone who had said earlier he wanted to talk more to me, he did not have much to say. He passed me the joint; I toted a few times and gave it back. As I was smoking, I noticed that he was inhaling the sugar. He said to me, "Have you ever done this before?" I said, "No, why would I want to inhale sugar?" He laughed. He said, "Here, try it." He took his pinky nail, which was the only long nail on his finger, scooped up a chunk, and put it to my nose. He held one nostril closed and then did it to the other. At first I did not feel a thing, then within minutes, my body went numb and I felt very vulnerable. The initial feeling made me want more, so I did. After about thirty minutes of this, he turned the lights off but left the television on, laid me down on my back, and took off my pants. I could not move; I did not know where I was or what was going on. He began to perform oral sex on me. After a few minutes, he stood up took the rest of his clothes off, placed a condom on his penis, and before I knew it. He had me in a position that up until that day, I had only done with a female. I did not feel any pain—my body was so numb and catatonic—but I cried anyway. It was then that I realized what was happening to me, as the tears rolled down the side of my face. I was being raped! I just pictured my mom and my new dad, my brothers and sisters, my grandparents, and my life as I once knew it before that moment. I wanted to go back in time. I wished I had not stopped on that bridge.

He was much stronger than I was, and I was clearly in no condition to try to run anywhere. I just waited until it was over. It went on for a long while—it seemed like hours, and to be honest, it was. *Dear God, why me?* When it was over, I lay there for a few minutes, quiet, until he dozed off. As he slept, I tried to get dressed so I could escape, but as I was pulling the door open, he woke up. He said, "Hold on, Sammy, don't go out there like that." I said, "I have to go or my grandparents will call my job to see if I have left already." I was very dizzy and confused about what had just happened to me. He said, "Let me walk you downstairs and make sure you get into a cab safely." He hailed the cab, gave the driver my address, and placed in my hand five crisp twenty-dollar bills. He said, "Pay him, and the rest is for you." He wrote his number on a piece of paper and told me to call him when I got in. I looked back as the cab was turning left to go down the hill to the bridge, and I noticed he was hailing a cab for himself. I did not call him when I got home; I just took a shower, went in my room, and closed the door behind me. I knew then that I was a changed person forever.

The next day I was sore in my bottom area as well as coming down from a high I had never experienced before. I had to still get up for school and be the good kid I was known to be. During lunch, I went to a payphone in the main entrance of the school, and I called the number he had given me. He said he was worried and wondered why I had not called last night. I said I was cool. I asked him what was that stuff he had given me; he said it was cocaine and told me to never do it around nobody but him. I thought I never wanted to do it again. I asked Vance his age, and he became silent. I asked again, "How old are you, man?" He finally said, "Thirty-six." I was shocked; my momma was only thirty-six. I said to him, "You are old enough to be my dad, man." He said, "Sammy, don't ever tell anyone about this. He asked me what I did with the money. I said, "I put it between my mattresses." The money was what I made in a week working in Manhattan, $90. Hiding large sums of money given to me from Vance became common practice. He asked if he could see me again; he claimed he missed me already. I told him to let me think about it. A week went by, and I never called him and had no intentions of it. My life seemed to be falling back into its normal place. At first, I felt like everyone that looked at me could tell what had happened. My girlfriend at the time did say that I seemed distant when we were together. I told her that I just had a lot on my mind, which was no lie. One day as I was leaving school, my buddies and I all noticed this black shiny Olds '98 in front of the school. The windows were tinted, so we could not tell who was in it. As I walked down the Grand Concourse alone because my buddies all took the bus or subway, I noticed this black ride following me. When it got closer, the windows came down, and the voice shouted out, "Sammy!" I looked out to the street, and it was him. I walked over to the car. He said, "Get in, I'll give you a ride home." I told him no. He said that he needed to talk to me. I had other questions for him, but at the moment, I just wanted to leave well enough alone. He said, "Boy, get your mother——— a——— in this car before I get a ticket." His harshness shook me up, but all I could do is remember him saying on the bridge that he would never hurt a cool young brother like myself. And although the next day I did feel pain from that experience, it went away by the end of the day. So I got in. He asked why I did not call him back. I said I had no reason to. He asked me if I was hungry. I said yes, so instead of dropping me off, we went to Sylvia's on Lenox Avenue. Vance had a way of getting his way. He told me he wanted me to know that he could not stop thinking about me and that he hoped that I did not tell anyone. I asked him whom I could tell. Did he not realize that he had just stripped me of my manhood? And how would I? I was now, in my mind, ashamed and afraid of the dude. After we were done eating, we walked up 125th and stopped at A. J. Lester clothing store. He said he wanted to buy me a gift. I knew this meant for me to keep my mouth shut. Grandpa had already practiced that technique with me. He spent over $500 on me, and all I had was a shirt, a pair of pants, a sweater, and a jacket. He said I needed to begin to dress more adultlike. I went to private school; we wore neckties and sports jackets every day. How adult is that? When we walked out, the guy said to him, "Yo! Vance, that's a good one right there." Vance replied, "I know, and get up off it." *No, they are not referring to me*, was all that came to my mind. I felt like a trophy, and not at all in the good sense of the word. Somehow, I felt like I was becoming a part of a world that I never knew existed. Vance was a drug dealer and very well-known in the area. I have to admit, I was a bit intrigued by his sense of power and position. He asked me if I needed anything else; I said I didn't need these. He said, "Yeah, you need something, and he took me to Men's Walker just up the street and let me pick out a pair of leather and suede British Walkers to complete my outfit. He took me home and asked me again to call him. I said what if I did not. He said, "I know where you live and where you go to school—what do you think would happen?" I walked off, and he called me back. He said, "Here." He handed me two one-hundred-dollar bills and a bag of weed. He said, "You might see something else you might like." I took it and went inside. My mattress was starting to become more valuable than it was worth.

Time went on, and I did not hear from him, and I did not call. What was strange was it was right after he threatened me to call, and I simply took the chance and did not call. *It's been a month, have I rid myself of this stranger and monster?* He was scary to me as well, once I got a chance to really look at him in character as well as appearance. On the day we were shopping, I heard him speak more; he had a deep and intimidating voice. Imagine Barry White 150 lbs. lighter, with a bodybuilder's build and eyes that seemed to look through you. I was a child and very afraid, yet intrigued by the boldness of this individual, his ability to command a room when he walked in, even if he did not say a word. I wanted to be that way. What I did not want to be was gay. But somehow it felt right for me. I loved being with Michaunda, but I did not feel emotionally attached to her, only during sex.

Vance was not feminine in any way. He was nothing like the way television depicted gay men; the stereotypical image of flamboyant, obnoxious, and feminine character did not apply to him. He was tough, like my dad or tougher. However, Vance never called. And then out of the blue, just when I was becoming a teenager again, three and a half months later, he reentered my life. I saw his car parked in front of my school as I was changing classes one afternoon. After class, I walked back over to the stairwell to see if he was there because I was afraid to go out. He was not there. I left school, still feeling a little strange. I decided to pass through the park. I did not go through this park often. It was an adult pick-up park. Everyone in the neighborhood knew that. Especially at night, I was always intimidated by this park, but I had a whole family that lived in the vicinity of the park. My family seemed to like the Bronx and Brooklyn, and we loved to live close to one another, but far enough that you may have to drive or walk for a minute. I remember one night, I cut through after a basketball game at my school, and as I was passing over the hill that led to a stairway, there was a tall, skinny guy and this really fat girl bent over doing it. They did not even stop at the sight of me walking by.

As I approached my grandparents' building, there stood Vance at the entrance of the building, and approaching from the other side of the street was my grandmother with two bags in her hand. I was relieved and scared because I did not know if Vance was there to harm me. I approached the building. He called out to me as I passed him by to meet my grandmother with her bags. "Samuel! Hey, Samuel! Li'l nigga, you hear me calling you?" My grandmother was luckily far enough not to have heard him. However, his body gestures toward me made her question me anyway. I took her bags and proceeded to the building. As he was walking away, she asked, "Sammy, baby, was that man saying something to you?" I said he asked me if I knew someone that lived in the building. Grandma was no fool. She looked me in the eye and said, "Hmmm hunh! Okay, Sammy! You'd better mind! Hear?" That meant "You'd better listen to what we tell you about strange people in this city," as they had always talked to us children about. They were among a first generation of our people to leave South Carolina by way of the Bahamas ancestry. Although our family was very large there, our roots were taking a strong hold in New York as well, and we needed to learn our "roots" before we "branched" out, so to speak. Well, I did the opposite of all four of my siblings; I grew a tree, branched out, sprouted leaves, then learned of my roots. And believe me, sometimes that sequence can cost you years of prosperity, and I don't mean in just money. You prosper when you finish college, you prosper when you raise a family, you prosper when you are just serving and doing things for the Lord. I learned that early in life. But this was a hindrance to my prosperity. The very next day after school, there he was. I did not want him to make a scene. I just felt that with his mentality, he was probably more than capable. I mean on the real, Vance was a full-grown thug who missed his youth because he spent most of that time in prison. His mentality did not grow up; that's why he was attracted to me a child. I walked over to his car; he let the window down, and he said, "Get in." As I got into the car, I noticed a few of my friends who, by the way, lived in Harlem. One of them was a senior. I had always admired the way he dressed. He seemed the most troubled by the sight of me leaving in the mysterious black Olds '98. Anyway, Vance pulled off quicker than I could get the door closed. He said that he did not appreciate me dissin' him yesterday, and if my grandmother had not been there, he would have snatched my little ass up! I said to him, "If she were not there, I would not have had to ignore you." He never liked my sarcasm, especially when I seemed more intelligent than he or when it came to deductive reasoning. He said, "Nigga, you a crazy little brother! You always gotta get the last word, *don't you*?" He yelled. I

33

was nervous but for some reason, not as intimidated as I thought I would be. I was not done, and for some reason, I felt that I had the most to say because he was the one that popped up out of nowhere, with all this new drama in my life. I asked Vance why after three months of not being around me, not trying to come to my school or call on the phone, he just popped up trippin' like he'd been here all along. He said he was locked up and that he got locked up that night, after he left me. I told him that was what he got for threatening me. I was never afraid to let someone know that I was still a child of the King. Vance was picked up for drug possession, but evidently, he did not have to stay long. I wished he were locked up for life. He asked me about the dudes that were watching me get into the car at the school. I expressed to him that some of them I was cool with, and a couple of them were seniors whom I just spoke to in passing. He said he recognized one of them and left it at that. Vance took me over to his house for the first time. He said it was time for me to learn more of him. He did not classify what we were, so I just assumed we messed around; however, it began to seem more like a relationship. To this day, however, I have never called it that. I knew that I may have been the main one but not the only one he dealt with sexually. We arrived at this beautiful brownstone on the lower east side of Harlem. The brownstones next to it were okay, but his just looked like it was remodeled. We walked inside, and he opened the first level to show it to me, and it was set up like a lounge with tables and chairs and a bar. He had art all over the place. It was wonderful. He said that he entertained at times and also let some of his peeps from the industry hold sets there. I came to meet several celebrities through Vance over time. Then he escorted me upstairs to the third level. He said that his brother rented the bottom level from him. We went upstairs; he opened the door, and my eyes fell in love. It was definitely the type of place I would like to have. He had expensive furniture, a large color television, a VCR. His stereo system was magnificent. I felt like I was with a low-key rich guy. He dimmed the lights, pulled me toward him, and said, "Samuel, I can give you so much, but you love me so little." I told him that that was not an emotion that I had ever felt for another male, and I don't believe that I ever could. He said, "I'll make you love me," then he turned around, slid a mirror from the mantle of the fireplace, then handed me that white powder again. I had school the next day, and also, I had already told my grandmother I was off that day. After the first few bumps, I did not care. Vance and I got high. He repeated our first night; only this time, I wanted it. I also wanted to find out more about his world. I was now closer to seventeen and about to enter into senior year. Vance did not like my sarcasm, but I knew it was the only thing that he would let me get away with because I was just being myself. I told him that I thought that he was weak because he had to get me high to do his dirty deed. I felt that now it was time for him to find out how smart I really was, so I began to pick his brain. I now, for some reason, had more control under the influence. I was able to say yes or no, hold a conversation, and decide when I had enough and when I was ready to go. I asked Vance if he enjoyed young boys like me because we were small and made him feel as though he were with a petite woman. He said that he had never been with anyone my age before and that I was the exception to of his rules. The other being that no one else would get his money or his love. Anyway, those words were lies. After debating with him for two hours and blowing his high as he put it, he walked downstairs and hailed me a cab. It was 12:00 a.m. I knew I was in for it. He handed me a card in an envelope and said, "Don't open it until you get home." Of course I did not listen, and the underside of the envelope said, "I knew you were going to open it and not listen. That is just your way of getting the last word." I chuckled because it was true. I was beginning to become fond of this attention and friendship. I opened the card, and of course there was money, $500 to be exact, and a letter in which he wrote:

Sammy,

I am sitting here in jail, ten days away from coming home. I have thought about you every day since I have been gone, wondering if you think of me. Sorry that I did not have a lot of time with you. Sorry that I did not leave you with enough information about me and how I felt about you. Always respect the man you are becoming. Yes, Sammy, man. I want you to always remember no matter what, you are first and foremost a man. Don't ever let anyone disrespect your manhood because of how you get down sexually, you know. I know you are a good kid and different from me. I don't want to change your world. I just want you to share mine. Sammy, this lifestyle is not easy. You are a good-looking brother, and there are going to be many who are going to want to enter your world. Don't let them take advantage of your precious heart. The first time I saw you, you were prettier than or just as pretty as any of the women I had ever been with. I just had to have you, feel your skin, smell your scent, and make love to you like no one ever had. Whatever you need, there is no need to ask—it's yours. Just say the word, and if anyone ever put their hands on you, I swear unto all that is holy, I will kill them! I want to protect you and make you the happiest person you can be. Sammy, when I get home, I am going to give you something to hold for me. It means a lot to me if you hold on to it in case anything should ever happen to me. If you had this, Sammy, I would not be sitting in here today. It is a key to my safe deposit box and my attorney's phone number. There is $500,000 in there in cash, stocks, and bonds. If you play your cards right, Sammy, that will pay for your college next year. I can't mail this letter to you as I would like to. They read the mail around here, man, and if it got out that I was kickin' it with a young dude, I may end up some nigga's bitch up in here, yo! And get more time to think about it! I will give it to you the first day I see you in person. Like I said, they read our mail before they send it out. Your young ass will cause me to get some more time. I care about you, li'l man, and damn, I think you gonna

35

be the one to make me fall in love and settle down from this game, son. Damn, now I'm in here crying, and shit, listen, I gotta go. Peace aiight!

Your Nigga,
Vance

By the time I was done reading the letter, we were at my grandparents' place and the driver was already paid by Vance, so I slid the five one-hundred-dollar bills in the envelope along with the card and placed it in my book bag before I got out of the car. It was too late to be stupid. This was the South Bronx. I opened the door and damn! My grandma didn't give me time to think. She just blew up. "Sammy, I don't know what you are out there doing, but you'd better mind! They're killing and raping y'all young people out there! You heard about what that man did in Atlanta with those twenty-one kids! You know it was not right that you did not call here. Call your mama, everybody all worried, and we could not even report you missing 'til tomorrow. If you are gonna be hanging out in the street then you gonna have to live with your momma because I'm not gonna have it in my house. My children did not do it, and neither will you." Now she already knew I knew better; I was a chip off the old block if anything. They all did a little bit of stuff growing up. I am proud of my aunts' and uncles' success today, but they were all hell on wheels when they were younger, all ten of them. My momma now on the other line and both of them were going off at the same time, blowing what was left of the high that was already coming down on me

I just blew up! I said, "If y'all will both give me a word in edgewise, I will tell you where I have been." I had not yet thought of an excuse, so I should have just let them keep talking. What in the world was I thinking? They both became silent. My mother said, "Then where the hell were you?" I could not speak. I threw the phone down and got up; I walked out the door of my grandmother's room, and I hollered out, "Guess!" I went into my room and closed the door. For some reason, all that drama did not bother me. I figured I had nearly a thousand dollars between my bed mattress, much weed in my closet, and an older dude who was all into me. I began to change from being this humble, quiet but assertive church kid to this sarcastic smart ass that grew up into a man overnight. The next day, I could barely get up for school, but I knew if I did not, my grandma would have immediately said I was drunk or suffering from a hangover. At lunchtime, one of the guys that had observed Vance pick me up last semester approached me. His name was Leslie. He asked if he could speak with me in private. I looked at him as though he was someone else trying to step to me, and quite honestly, I don't know if I would have minded that. My interest in the same sex was now piqued. However, he was really coming to warn me, but I did not listen. He said, "Yo, Sammy, I ain't tryin' to be in your business, but that cat that rolled up in here, you don't need to mess with." He said that if I continued, the longer I was with him, the harder it would be to get away. I asked him if he knew him from his neighborhood; he said yes and no. He said he lived in upper Harlem, and he had kicked it with Vance for two years from the time he was fourteen until he was sixteen. I remembered seeing him when he was a sophomore and a junior and he was well-dressed and, come to think of it, sort of had the attitude that I was now displaying. He talked to me every day after that. He questioned the money, the drugs, and the sex. Leslie told me that he would help me plan my escape. Vance had told me that there was never anyone like me when actually, there were several more before me, according to Leslie. This guy was only fourteen, and Vance had been thirty-three years old at that time. A part of me wanted to escape, but the materialistic child inside said I was gonna ride this horse until I said "Whoa!" Well, after thousands of dollars and many more outfits and, of course, champagne and cocaine, "Whoa!" came in two forms of destruction. The first was when I decided to visit Vance one day unannounced and he did not hesitate to let me in; however, when I walked in, to my surprise, there was another dude sitting at his kitchen table and they were doing something very strange-looking to me. He told me to go in his living room and that he would be right there. From the living room was a wall mirror that gave me full view of what was going on. They were shooting heroin. My heart started beating fast, and I was just about to panic, when Vance and the guy came out of the front real slow like. Vance leaned over me and said, "I don't ever want you doing this shit, you hear me?" He then pulled out a pipe and placed this hard beige substance inside, pulled on it with the lighter in front of him, and then he handed it to the other guy. Then he smoked on it. Now I know what crack smells like. Vance was so high I just looked at the two of them, and right before my eyes, they began to have sex. I was hurt but also surprised that Vance did not respect me being in the same room. I went to the door, looked back at the sight of these two individuals who were too high to even realize that they were not even in the room themselves, and I left. As I was leaving the building, Vance's brother was approaching. I believe he noticed the horror on my face. He asked me if I needed to talk; I told him no. I knew that he wanted to get with me anyway because Vance had told me that they had arguments regarding me before, so I definitely was not going there with this cat. I was now becoming very afraid and leery of this world that Vance had introduced me to. His brother did not have the money or the clout that Vance had; however, Vance was on a spiral down and I could see it. Two days later, he popped up at my school again, and to his surprise, Leslie and I were standing out front talking to each other. Leslie asked me not to go near him. I felt that a scene was about to take place; I had told Leslie right before Vance pulled up about the drug incident. Leslie really wanted to protect me, but I think that he was also somewhat afraid. Leslie said that it was up to me; I could just keep walking or I could get in the car. I chose to walk. Leslie walked me home and hung out with me for a while. I did not think Vance was going to pull off without making trouble, but he did. I knew it was not over though. Before Leslie left to head home, he stood up, turned to me, and gave me a hug. Although he was seventeen, almost eighteen, he seemed older, like me. But he looked older than I did. Leslie held me longer than I thought he should have, and then it happened—we kissed. His tongue was sweet and soft. I had not felt that before this time, only with a female. Leslie pulled away, looked at me, and said, "I have always liked you." I told him that I was not ready to go there with him. And I never did. But I wanted to.

I just thought that maybe Vance had done something to me that turned me off from other guys. I wish that really was the case because it nearly cost me my life one night, being attracted to another guy in his presence. The second leap toward destruction happened a couple of months after the drug incident. He began to call me, apologizing and crying to me over and over again. By this time, I had my own phone, and he would call me every day, all night, until I would decide to see him. He arrived at my home behind the building one evening and honked his horn. I looked out and noticed that it was Vance. I did not want to go, but I did not want my grandma to hear him constantly honking and decided to go look from the living room window. So I told her I was going over to my buddy's house, and I left. As Vance and I were pulling off, I looked up at the window, and my grandmother was staring directly at me. It broke my heart to see the expression of fear and disgust on her face. I looked at Vance and asked him if he minded if I go back to the house. He told me, "Hell yeah, I mind," and drove faster. He said that he planned a special night and wanted me to get any and everybody else out of my head, that it was his time now. We went to his home; on the bed were ten one-thousand-dollar bills in the shape of the letter *S*, a fur coat with a hood, and a two-piece leather suit. Right then and there, I knew I that had gotten too deep into his world. I thought it was an awful lot of money, looking at ten thousand dollars lying on that bed. And when I mentioned that to Vance, he said, "Shit, that ain't nothing—the fur coat alone cost more than that." He said it was a custom-made one-of-a-kind Japanese Tanuki, designed by him for me, and that was supposed to be my Christmas, birthday, and graduation present in November. He said, "Nigga, that coat cost me over fifteen Gs. You better act like you know!" Vance had a way of making you feel guilty about his need to give, give, and give. I could not explain this to my family. How was I supposed to wear this coat that was a quarter of my Dad's salary? I did not know what a Tanuki was, but I bet he did. I did the extended version at my grandparents', and since Grandpa had recently passed on, my grandma needed me there with her. She, on the other hand, accepted the fact that it was a fake coat. But she kept saying, "Sammy, I know you say that coat is fake, but it sure looks like a real something to me." Now Grandma was one of those people who allowed you to come to her. If you lie to her and she knows you're lying, she waits patiently until the truth unfolds for itself, then she tells you, "I knew it was so." Well, I did not keep the coat very long anyway. That New Year of 1985 set something for me. It was the turn of my life, and I wanted to become a liberated man free to broaden his learning horizons and become a viable asset to our society. It was, I believe, the third Thursday in January, and by this time, Vance had offered a buddy of his who owned a nightclub in Harlem to be his bouncer for a few nights while his regular guy was out of town. Vance agreed. He asked me to come out and keep him company by the door one of the nights, so on Thursday, I did. This place was a well-known bar in Harlem called Andre's, and on certain nights, it catered to gay clientele. I walked in, and sitting right on the opposite side of the door was Vance. I was dressed to the hills. I had on a pair of Guess jeans with the leather crotch, the leather sweater he had bought me, a pair of black leather and suede British Walkers which he also bought, and of course, the Tanuki. The room seemed to have stopped

CHURCH BOY IN THE DARK

at my very sight, and in slow motion, all eyes were on me. Vance caught the reaction of the whole room right away. The door closed behind me; he pulled me toward him like some bitch and then began trying to stick his tongue down my throat. I was never one for public displays of affection, especially with no dude. I pulled away and said, "Chill." He said, "Oh! You've got on my shit and gonna try and play post with me!" My eyes popped out of my head, and I cocked my head to the side in amazement at the way he was loud-mouthing me in front of people. I said, "Vance, just respect me in public, that's all. I ain't trying to go there with you, just chill." I took off my coat and pulled up a bar stool. I sat there and talked to him for about thirty minutes, then he handed me a folded ten-dollar bill. He directed me to the restroom and told me to use a stall. It was, of course, cocaine. I took a few bumps then went back to my seat near the door. About another thirty minutes later, I started getting cold, so Vance told me to sit at the bar. His friend and owner fixed me a drink. I sat there for about ten minutes when this real sexy thugged-out cat came and sat next to me. He made eye contact then winked. I just turned my head. Obviously, he had missed the preview at the door. He told the bartender to give me another one of what I was drinking, then he introduced himself to me. He said, "Hey, I'm Gregg." I said "What's up," and I thanked him for the drink. Gregg was tall, much taller than Vance but not as built, and he had this look in his eye like he was not scared of anything. He was very well-dressed and pulled out a knot so thick I could have wallpapered my room with it. He wrote his number on a matchbook and slid it to me. He walked off, and maybe two minutes later, Vance was in my ear whispering, "If I catch you talking to that sneaky-ass dude again, I'm gonna mess you up!" Up to that point, he had never hit me but definitely made threats. He was becoming more possessive, and as I said, his life was going downhill because of his excessive drug use. His business was slowing down, and I could see that his drug using was eating most of the profit. Gregg came back over. I liked him. He was very handsome and spoke very well, although his appearance would have made you think otherwise. I then gave him my number. For the first time, I had met someone that I thought was cool, and he was considerably younger than Vance; he was only twenty-four. Vance walked over again; this time, he and Gregg got into it. The altercation quickly escalated! Gregg grabbed a glass from the bar and slammed Vance in the forehead with it. Vance grabbed him by his ears, and while he dug his nails into him, he kneed him in the stomach. I tried to grab Vance at that point. He threw Gregg to the ground, turned around, then punched me in the face, grabbed me by the neck, then commenced to pulling me toward the door; he grabbed the coat then threw me out into the snow. He pulled out his gun and pointed it at me lying on the ground. He said if I was going to protect some other nigga over him, then I needed to get away from him—fast. I took off everything I had on. I must have been crazy. The whole bar had come outside. I threw the fur in the middle of the street as cars drove over it. I broke the gold and diamond necklace off me and threw it at him, and I threw the shoes at him. I told him that if he ever came near me again, I would kill him myself. I ran to the corner of 125th Street to flag down a cab. I walked another block to get away from the area. A silver BMW pulled alongside of me; it was Gregg. He got out of the car, opened his trunk, and handed me a leather bomber to put on. He gave me the shoes on his feet, which were three sizes bigger than mine, and he put me in his car. He asked me where I lived and commenced to taking me home. His ears were dripping with blood, and his lip was swollen. I said to him, "Thank you for helping me get home in this cold," but I did not feel that I deserved his courtesy because I got him into this fight. He said that I did not do it; being in the game did. And he felt like the winner because the prize was sitting next to him. Here went that trophy syndrome again. He said that if he had to, he would take another ass whippin' for my honor but no time soon. We both laughed. After that day, Gregg and I went to Rutger basketball games at the Polo Grounds, Knicks games at the Garden, plays on Broadway, and so much more. He exposed me to culture. And you guessed it—love. I fell in love with Gregg, and also with myself.

Straddling the Fence . . . Which Life Is Mine?

The Third Chapter

Well, Gregg and I ended up having a two-year relationship. He somehow, in spite of his street lifestyle, was a good influence on me to achieve my goals and be successful. I did not get high like I used to. I was working on Wall Street for a securities firm as a computer operator and attending Pace University in the area. Gregg and his drug-slinging scene were beginning to be too much for me to be around, although he protected me as though he were my bodyguard. Then one sad day, I woke up and began to cry out for what seemed no reason at all. I felt like a part of me was torn off. I immediately called Gregg's home. His sister answered the phone. They all knew what time it was with us and loved me like one of theirs. She cried into the phone, "Sammy, someone shot Gregg! Gregg is gone, he is dead!" Deep down, I felt that Vance had something to do with it. While I was not present, they actually had three or four more altercations since that last time, so their feud never ended. It was beginning to seem like I was never going to have sanity in my life; from age sixteen to nineteen it had been nothing but drama. I wanted to do something in honor of Gregg's death, so I decided to pursue a career in singing and acting. Gregg was fond of the arts, and I learned to appreciate it immensely due to his being supportive and not disruptive in my life. I still continued to sing with the guys in the group. To be honest with you, I never stopped, even through the times with Vance. Gregg made it easier to be faithful and dependable to the group; he even came out to hear us sing a few times. He always said he loved my voice. He left me with many treasures to carry me through the rest of my life. He also left me with the person closer to him than I ever thought I could be, his best friend, Miguel, who over time actually became my best friend. Miguel was a sexy black Panamanian brother whom I guess felt the need to take me under his wing. He used to tell me about all of the things Gregg would say about me, most of all how I was going to be the one to make him want to change his life and leave the street game. He said that he had never heard Gregg speak of anyone in that manner, not even his baby's mother. Gregg did not keep me in the dark about his feelings from day one, so I knew that what Miguel was saying was true. I did find love and, at that point, realized that it was possible. However, as I told Miguel, I wanted to date women and to someday be married with children. So I left dudes alone for a long time. Michaunda, as you might have guessed, tapered off once prom was over. It was hard to convince her that I was not selling drugs for someone by the way we were taking OJs (fancy taxis) and eating in fine restaurants as teenagers. Vance's in and out moments gave me ample time to also spend with Michaunda. Now I wanted to spread my new lovemaking talents around with a few other women. Michaunda was a true church girl, but each church girl has a wild side, I assumed. So I dated a lot of women from different churches in different boroughs around the city. A few of them I was able to hit (have sex with), and a few of them had combination locks on those things with no combination numbers to get in it. There was this one female—her name was Gina. She was fine as all the heavens and the earth. When she smiled, her eyes seemed to begin to glisten and her body just molded her shape into her clothing. I wanted her badly. She was, as the church would classify her, a prophetess. I respected that, especially when she called out my alternative sexuality. But Gina was a cool sister. I was still in college and, at this point, twenty-one years old. She was twenty-five, very mature, and yes, seeking marriage. Because of her status, I was afraid to approach her with the idea of sex, but I wanted to so bad. We had been dating by this point for four and a half months. Usually by now, I would have had it ten to thirty times. I had become as good in bed with women as I became with men. It was a sport to see if I could satisfy my partner to certain levels. I guess to me that is what makes the monogamous relationship a novelty every time. If I wanted to hear my name, I brought certain things into the moment. If I wanted to hear a person call out the name of God, I brought an added spiritual appeal to the level of lovemaking, going higher and higher until you climaxed. I said all that to say this: I was really ready to show this to Gina. We had a few close calls and some closer calls. Until finally, eight months after we met, I was over her home one evening, and she and I began to discuss a little about my past with dudes. She made me throw away any pictures I had of Vance, and she wanted me to throw the pictures of Gregg away, but I could not. She asked me to promise her that I would never leave her for a man, or another woman for that matter. I promised. I was naturally a faithful-relationship type of person anyway, so that part would be easy. I was making good money working full time on Wall Street and going to school. The company I worked for even had tuition reimbursement, so I kept a 3.3 average or better so I could get 100 percent tuition back. I drove a BMW, and thanks to Gina, I was a very sharp dresser in suits and ties. She was always sharp. She wore designer hats, carried designer bags, and wore the finest clothing. Gina was a certified public accountant for a Fortune 500 company and very well off. We made a very good-looking and positive couple. On our tenth month, Gina's twenty-sixth birthday came; I felt that at this point she probably really wanted to know where she stood with the man in her life. I called Miguel up and told him that I had intentions of proposing. Miguel did not think I was ready nor did he feel that I wanted to be with women exclusively. I shared with Miguel that I had become accustomed to living a certain lifestyle and that anybody with me had to meet a standard so I could maintain a certain standard of living. Miguel asked if I was going to buy her a ring. I said yes, for her birthday. He asked if he was going to be my best man; I said of course. Although I could tell he was not happy with my decision, he stayed by my side through it all. He kept me away from the gay lifestyle that he was a part of. I knew of it but did not experience the clubs and parties yet. Miguel had a friend who managed a jewelry store in the diamond district in Manhattan. Of course, knowing Miguel, it was somebody he had a "shing" with, as he called it—short for a shoddy fling, go figure. When we first walked into the store, I could tell the guy was happy to see Miguel and even more happy to see what he had with him. He nearly took my hand off squeezing it so hard for juice or something. His name was Dartanian. He was also from Panama but not very handsome. Miguel said to me where his good looks were I would never see. Miguel said he had trade. That meant a big penis. I did not care anymore; I just wanted a ring. I had $3,500 to spend. Miguel said that he could make Dartanian sell me a $4,500 ring for $2,500. I did not believe him, so I tested it. I picked out this beautiful 3½-carat marquis cut with baggets along the side; it was a huge rock. It was selling for $4,700. Miguel asked me if that was the one I wanted. I said yes. He told Dartanian something in his ear, and then we left. Miguel said for me to give him the $2,500 and that he would be over my house tonight with the ring. Miguel and I hung out for a while, got something to eat, then I got on the Metro North train and headed home. He said that he was heading to Brooklyn to meet Dartanian at his house. He had to be there by 6:30, he said. I did not like this, but I wanted this ring. Gina reminded me of a first lady, and she was definitely about to be mine. I felt like my true life was about to begin. I could leave all that mess behind me. I smiled nearly all the way home, picturing our wedding day and our new home in Long Island. Around 10:00 p.m., Miguel called me and asked me to meet him in the Village. Miguel did not like taking the subway, and I knew he definitely was not going to ride from Brooklyn to the North Bronx if he did not have to. I asked him to meet me in Times Square instead. He said, "Yeah, my bad, I hear you." The Village was considered the alternative lifestyle mecca, and rightfully so. It was filled with heritage, culture, reality, and art. I picked him up. He got in the car, leaned over, kissed me on my cheek, popped open the ring, and said, "Sammy, my darling, will you marry me?" My mouth dropped. Then he handed me back $500 of my money. He said he kept $500 for himself for the hookup and that the guy only wanted $1,500 because he thought I was so cute. I was not complaining nor questioning, but I knew that was a pass at me to respond to. The next day, I called Gina at work and asked her where she wanted to go for dinner. Her birthday was the next day. She said for me to surprise her. I made reservations for Tavern on the Green in Central Park. I rented a limousine for the day, bought a bottle of Moet, and got dressed for a proposal she would never forget. I called her from a phone in the limo and told her I was around the corner and to come outside; her family was sitting out on the porch, just cackling as usual. She walked out, and I could see her from the distance as I was approaching, looking for my car. She was looking past the limo and just as exquisite as any queen on her way to the royal ball. As the driver began to stop in front of the house, he opened my door. I grabbed five dozen of roses in multicolors, and the ring, I opened it, and I began to sing, "You are so beautiful to me. You are everything I've hoped for, you are everything I've dreamed, oh *oooh*! You are so beautiful to meeeeee, marry meeeeeheeeee!" The neighbors by this point had come out; her mother stopped cackling and was bawling, in tears. Gina was just catatonic as she stared at the size of the rock from the distance she stood. I approached, kissed her forehead, and said, "Gina, please be my wife." She said, "Yes, now and forever." We arrived a little early for our reservation, so we took a carriage ride around Central Park. Her ring seemed to just light up the sky that evening. And the glow on her face made me feel like a great man. We began to plan our wedding the very next day. She was picking fabrics. We found the designer to make her gown. I found the designer to make my ensemble, and we were on our way. Two weeks before our wedding day and just two weeks away from our one year anniversary together, I received a phone call from a very good friend of Gina's and also one of her maids-of-honor. She said that she felt that it was only right that she told me. She and Gina rode the subway into work together every morning, and on this one particular morning, Gina had told her that she was in a BMW last night and would be in a Mercedes tonight. She said that she had questioned Gina on what she meant, and Gina had told her that she was going to make love to her ex-boyfriend one last time before she got married. I did not want to believe it. I paged Gina and called her on her cell phone; she did not respond to either. I got in my car and drove all the way out to Queens to her home; she was not there. But her mom did say with this weird look in her eye, "When she left earlier, I had assumed that you traded your car in for that Mercedes and just did not want to come in and say hello to me." I told her when Gina got in to tell her that I said the wedding was off! "If she wants to get married in two weeks, she can marry the guy with the Mercedes!"

Over 12,000 dollars had been spent for this day, most of which we could not recover. I was devastated. The night went on, and I did not hear from her until the very next day. She did not have a clue why I called the wedding off. She said that she and her sister were over her aunt's house working on the bridesmaid's gowns and she fell asleep. I was vicious and vulgar, which was just not in my character, because I could not believe what I was hearing. I told her that I hoped her aunt drove into her as well as she drove that Mercedes. She began to sob and asked how I knew. I never told her how. I just said "I know" and hung up. My parents were appalled. They had spent the majority of the money because her parents did not have that kind of money for what she desired in a wedding. My mom, the doctor, told us to spare no expense, and I knew she meant it. She made over $20,000 a month, so that was still reasonable to her. She was furious, though she said that she wanted Gina to pay her back and that she had better give me the ring back. Gina did refuse to give me back the ring, and I could have taken her to court, but I decided that her life was about to crumble anyway, so she could keep it. I thought that life was going to get better for me after this, and just when it did, this happened. I needed to move on somehow. Miguel was right there to pick up the pieces, but as many of my friends before, Miguel also felt the need to protect me. Miguel offered to take me out one evening to get me out of my slump. I picked him up, and off we went. He took me to my first gay club; it was called Better Days. I could not believe my eyes—men dancing with men, women dancing with women, and the interchange. I needed a drink. Miguel schooled me on the way there. He said, "Sammy, I am telling you now. You are my little brother if anyone asks, and they will ask. Be cool and don't be giving up any conversation to these queens." I said okay, and that was it. When we got in, he immediately took my hand and walked me to the dance floor. I loved to watch Miguel dance; he made me smile, and he was so smooth. He reminded me a lot of Gregg. Off to the side, watching us while we were dancing, was this Italian Marky Marc–looking guy staring at me, and Miguel noticed him. Miguel said, "Hell, no!" I said, "Why? He looks like a cool dude and he's cute." Miguel frowned upon interracial relations. I just felt people were people, like, love or hate, we are still people just the same. He was a bold, mysterious cat though. He came up to me on the dance floor and said, "When you are done, can I talk to you?" I looked at him. His lips were like wet but not dripping. His eyes were a bluish green. His hair was dark brown, and his skin was olive tone. I was amazed at this gorgeous dude checking me out. I told Miguel that I needed to at least get Gina off my mind so I wanted talk. The Italian guy's name was Johnny, Johnny De LaPrissi. He modeled in *GQ Magazine* and many others. We talked that night but did not meet again until later. I was still not ready to be intimately involved with anyone. I knew this was not the average white boy, and I was not ready for the action. The very next day, Miguel had plans for us to go to another club. I was not ready to see another, but staying at home was no longer an option. I had been the perfect church boy with my future wife for over a year, and she had flipped the script. So off we went to one of his favorites, Tracks. I liked this place—it was huge and well-lit in all the right places; you could see people better inside. I did not know that New York had so many fine black men. I no longer felt like I was this drop-dead gorgeous boy. Here people looked but never tried to approach me; there were just too many to get into one immediately, I assumed. Miguel said it was because I looked like the type of person that was unapproachable, when I was actually the complete opposite. I was a very pleasant person. However, I did adapt to being standoffish over time because of Vance's pressure to keep me to himself at the bar. Miguel walked off with this dude, told me he would be back, and went into the restroom. Like ten minutes later, they both came out. He came up to me sniffling. I knew then what he was doing. With Gregg, that was no longer in my life. Gregg did not use what he sold, nor did he like to be around anyone doing anything more than having a drink. So for some years now, that had been out of my life. I was concerned about the type of person Miguel really was becoming. Miguel was very good-looking, but I don't think he saw himself as worthy of having someone great in his life. That night, he came up to me and told me that he was not going back to the Bronx with me and that he would call me tomorrow. I said, "You came with me and you will leave with me." I wanted to know where he was going. He asked me if I would feel more comfortable if I dropped them off. I said of course I would feel better. I did not like the way this cat looked. He was sort of drugged out, and his clothes did not look very clean. For it to just be 3:00 a.m., he looked as though he had not been home in a couple of days. We pulled up in front of the brownstone apartment. It was in a nice neighborhood in Brooklyn called Clinton Hills. *Maybe this brother is about something, and just getting his hangout on.* They exited my car. I watched them go in so I could see exactly the door they entered, and then I left. I hated what I was thinking about Miguel. I wondered if my new friend was promiscuous and if he was going to try to bring me into that world. Miguel did just the opposite. He warned me of different people, places, and things in the life, as he called it. Miguel would never let anyone step to me in the clubs. They called us the Polo kids because we wore a lot of Ralph Lauren gear and hung out at the Polo Ground Rutger Games. We really became like brothers. To this day, I don't know how I completed college and went to work. We hung out at least three to four times a week. Miguel used to tell me that I should never do anything with anyone, not even a female, without a condom. He would say, "You cannot afford to have a baby or lose your life." He said that I was different from a lot of people in the life. He said that I had a chance to become successful and a positive role model for gay and bisexual men. I wanted the same for him, but he had this mentality that his life was doomed to destruction. I tried so hard to change Miguel, but Miguel had his own agenda. We hung out for about three years strong, and then he left and moved to Atlanta. I felt that he was making a mistake, but I could not stop him. During those three years, I was not totally committed to life with Miguel. I did contact Johnny De LaPrissi about one month after we met at Better Days. He said he thought I had forgotten about him. I should have. He was very strange yet intriguing, I learned a lot about his world. He had an apartment in Soho with a black female roommate. The first time I went over to his apartment was magical. He made me forget about color. Let's just say Italians are more black than we or they would care to believe. My second visit, however, was not as good. He also began to share with me that he was having financial problems and needed $2,000 to catch up on his bills. I had the money. Giving it to him would not have been a problem, except I did not know him. He told me that he had a friend who escorted for a living and that this friend could get him a few jobs that would help him. I did not have a clue what he meant by escorting until he showed me his friend's ad in the *Advocate* magazine. I was stunned that there was actually a publication geared to selling sex across the United States. He said that he had done it before when his modeling assignments were not coming in steady enough. I hated to see him have to prostitute himself, but I could not give this stranger my money. I did not know when I'd see him again from day to day. We were not in touch like that, and he did not seem responsible. He told me of the different celebrities that he had been with. Little did I know celebrities were about to enter my life all over again. I decided that Johnny was just going to be a shing and that I needed to move on. So I did. I began to sing again. In church, I sang background only—rarely did I lead—but I hit the secular open mic circuit across the city in the hopes of being picked up by a record label. I sang at Sweetwater's, Honeysuckles, S. O. B.'s Soul Kitchen, and Nell's, just to name a few. The gay club scene was fading fast for me. Miguel was not as enthused with straight people and their spots as I was. But even in the straightest of atmospheres, one can find what he or she desires most. I had grown up with a well-known hip-hop artist, and somehow, we began to hang out. He and his rap duo partner were doing very well in the early '90s, and of course, I was still a thug magnet, so he enjoyed my company. He invited me to many industry sets and to his record company; we even reviewed videos before they hit the market. Let's just call him Silky. One day, Silky called me up to come out to New Jersey and give him a ride to the label; it was champagne and cocaine all over again. We started doing cocaine that day as we began to hit the streets, and then later on that evening, we went to a well-known radio disc jockey's anniversary party in midtown. It was there that I met—we'll call him DL (short for Down Low). DL was a hot solo rap artist at the time and very, very fine. A couple of magazines were out there taking pictures for their next issue, and I ended up in one of them, *Word Up Magazine*, exactly. It included me, Silky, his partner, and another gentleman. DL approached. When we were done, he motioned to Silky to come his way. Silky and he walked off. I saw Silky shrug his shoulders as if he did not know the answers to DL's questions. Later on, Silky gave me a piece of paper with DL's private number on it. He said that he was interested in a male vocalist for one of his tracks on his new album. He said he needed someone who had that Colonel Abrams sound. That was definitely me. He wanted to try something new, calling it Hip House. I thought the concept was cool. As the night ended, I walked up to DL to speak to him about his intentions; he ignored me as though I was not even standing there. So I walked off. When I got outside, he ran behind Silky and me. He pulled the bottom portion of my jacket. He said, "Yo! Money! Why you stepped off like that?" I told him that I was no buster or herb and that I did not give a damn who he was or who he thought he was; I didn't stand off to the side and wait for no dude like I was his bitch before I was acknowledged. He chuckled. He said, "Damn yo! My fault." He looked at Silky and said, "I really like this dude." He turned to me and said, "Are you gonna call me tomorrow?" I nodded. I did not call, and two days later, my phone rang; it was DL. He said, "Damn, baby, I had to track a brother down." I said that I was busy. I also felt that he needed his ego deflated some. He invited me over to his house. I accepted the invitation. It was nice but not what you would think a celebrity making his loot would have. He said the label got most of his loot but not for long. He told me that he wrote all his material and that he was going to begin producing himself. He was smart, and I guess that is why he is so successful today. We had a few drinks and talked for a couple of hours. I could tell that he wanted to do something but did not know how to approach it. I wanted to get with him from day one; not only that, he was the first celebrity that ever showed interest in me. He rolled a blunt. As the blunt got smaller, I offered to give him a shotgun that would give our lips an opportunity to touch. He got the hint. DL removed the blunt from his mouth, blew out the smoke, then leaned over and began to kiss me with a passion that can only be described as true romance. I could not believe how sensitive and compassionate he was. He moved his hands all over my body as though he was caressing satin sheets. We made love for several hours. I did not want this night to end. Obviously he did not either, because as we reached that third and final moment of ecstasy, he asked if I would spend the night. I declined. I felt that the best thing for me to do was not to wake up the next day to a sober thug or B-Boy. If they were really into you and not the high that might have perpetuated the moment, then you can be assured they would call back the next day. Besides, I had a way of leaving a person so satisfied the first and last thing they think of when they do wake up the next day is that moment with me. Not to toot my own horn, but I was right. It was not just the alcohol and weed; it was the way I put it down. He let me know that when he called me at home, not too long after I left his house. DL said that he wanted to make sure that I got home safely and to also tell me that he had never been sexed to the level that we went to before with another dude. I then questioned the number of dudes there had been in his past. He said he had just maybe two experiences in life, I believed him, since I did most of the work. But damn, did he catch on quick. The following day, we had lunch. He went to the studio at his label after lunch, then we met for dinner. As much as I wanted to get down with him again, I decided to wait. That lasted seven days, then we were at it again. This time, he surprised me with—you guessed it—an extravagant gift. He gave me a diamond pendant set in gold of the letter *S* in the style of the Superman emblem. He said, "I am sure you can find a chain that you would like to go with this." I said, "I'm sure I can." A few moments later, he asked me to get him a beer out of the refrigerator. I opened the door to find a long gift-wrapped box. It was a diamond and gold chain but very subtle, more gold than diamond. I liked that it was more conservative like myself. He admitted that he wanted me to be his regular dude for that keep-it-on-the-low experience; however, he was still very much in love with his girlfriend, whom he said he would someday marry. I said, "Although we kicked it the way we did on the first night we were alone together, I do not want you to mistake me for some boy toy or permanent or temporary, for that matter, booty call." It was so hard for me to let him go, but I remembered the things that both Gregg and Vance instilled in me about first and foremost being a man and a man of dignity. He said he respected that. He gave me a tight hug and one last kiss that was so passionate and strong it brought tears to my eyes. I wished him luck in his career, then I left. My heart was so devastated because deep down inside, I wanted to go against my own morals and values. Time went on, and I continued to go to school and work. Right before my graduation from college, more tragedy struck. My brother Winston was dispatched to rush to a hostage situation in the South Bronx. The gentleman who was holding the persons hostage in the bank decided that he was going to open fire into the crowd from the roof. As my brother Winston ran to the aid of an officer who was shot, Winston himself was shot in the head. At that point for me, this was it. This was the straw that broke the camel's back. I had it with New York and was ready for change. I waited till after I received my degree, and I moved to Atlanta. Miguel was excited, and at first I thought it was the best move I could have ever made. Little did I know there was more devastation that was still to come into my life.

Leaving This Old World Behind Me, Still Trying to Find Me

The Fourth Chapter

Moving to Atlanta was great for the first month and a half. The city was preparing for the 1996 Olympics, so the energy was high. Miguel and I became roommates, I found a really good job, and I began attending one of the largest churches in the city, New Birth Missionary Baptist. Miguel had met a gentleman; his name was Mitch, who for some reason just could not believe that Miguel and I were just friends and had never been intimate before. I asked Mitch if he had sex with all his friends before they became friends, and he said yes; that's how he could tell if they were going to be friends or sex buddies. I said. "Well, you don't ever have to worry about you and me becoming friends." Right in the presence of Miguel, Mitch said, "Yeah right, until I get up in that fat ass of yours with your pretty self." I laughed and said, "I could tell by the way you keep looking down in my crotch you have no interest in my ass, but I am used to perpetrating tops like yourself. I takes good care of boys like you, son." Miguel and I burst out in laughter. I did not like him, nor did I appreciate him disrespecting my friend. Every day that I had the chance, I would stress to Miguel that I felt that Mitch was no good and probably just as promiscuous as the rest of the boys in this city. Miguel claimed that he was in love, so I left it alone. One evening, he and Miguel were up very late getting high on cocaine and, from what I could hear, having continuous sex. When I finally heard them quiet down, I retired to my bedroom where I could now get some sleep. About one hour later, I heard my room door open. I turned around, and standing in my door butt naked was Mitch. I said, "What the hell are you doing in my room? Get your black ass out!" He said, "Shut up before you wake Miguel." He began to get in my bed. He said, "That's the way we do it out here in the ATL. We share, baby." I said, "If you don't get your high ass out of my room, I am going to clock you." He did not believe me. Mitch was a big dude everywhere—big hands, big feet. He stood 6'4" and had a penis that met the middle of his thighs. He grabbed me by my arms, got on top of me, and tried to pull my underwear down. I went ballistic. I said, "Yo! Nigga, I ain't one of these Atlanta freaks." I kneed him in the groin, ran to wake Miguel, and would you believe, my best friend turned on me. He accused me of coming on to him. I said, "If I was coming on to him, how come he is in my room holding his nuts?" When Miguel confronted him, he did not even have the decency to admit that he tried to rape me. I told Miguel, "If this is the type of cat you want to call your lover, you can have him." They went into Miguel's room and argued for a while, and then I heard them having sex all over again. I was really disgusted. As I said, Miguel never knew his worth and always settled for less. The next day, I went into the leasing office and told them that I would like to come out of my lease and move into a one-bedroom. They agreed, since Miguel had actually been in the apartment before I got there. I was not bound by the lease, just an occupant. Three days later, I began to pack and break down my bedroom suit. Miguel asked me why we could not work it out. I said, "Miguel, if you want to stay with Moby Trick Dick, that is on you. But I don't have to." I could see the hurt in his face, but then I could also see that Miguel was angry with me for leaving him. About one month later, I was preparing to leave for work, and when I went outside, my BMW was gone. I rushed over to Miguel's apartment; there was no answer. I went to the leasing office, and they said that they did not have any reason to have it towed so they do not know what might have happened. I called the police and did a police report. For some strange reason, after that day, Miguel strayed away from me. He lost his apartment, getting high with Mr. Moron Mitch, and since he never had a car, I did not know how he was going to make it. If Miguel would have not let that jerk move in with him, I would have been glad to help him with his rent. It was not like I had not sent him money from New York prior to my moving, so I already knew that he was not being very responsible with his finances. Miguel stopped speaking to me, and it broke my heart; we were not just friends, but we were like brothers as well. We did not speak again until after a year. I did meet a few guys, but there was no one that I would even let tie my shoes, let alone sleep with me. It was not because they were not attractive, but the character and standards of these individuals were so low I could not see degrading myself. So I decided to date a female. I went to all the straight hangouts and had a ball. Ironically, while waiting to get my haircut at this unisex beauty and barber salon in College Park, there walked in this lovely, sexy vision of womanhood. She looked at me as though to say, *Boy, what are you staring at?* I just had to make a comment. I said to her, "See, I was gone tell you how beautiful you were until you made that ugly face." She sucked her teeth and walked off. She must have gotten there just in time for her appointment because she went straight to the chair. The whole time she sat, she kept looking my way. I could tell she and her stylist were having a discussion about me. After my cut, I got up and walked out to my brand-new BMW. She came out with a shampoo cap on her head and said, "So you're just gone leave like that and not say anything?" I said, "What should I say? I don't know you." And I made an ugly face, turned my head, and sucked my teeth like a female. She laughed hard then said, "Obviously, you don't want to know me with attitude," and she began to walk away. I immediately turned back toward her and said, "I did not say all that now, let's not get crazy." She came down to where I was, pulled her car keys out of her pocket, and lo and behold, a BMW. She said, "Walk me to my car, soldier." Other than the color, our cars were twins; parked right next to me was her car. She went inside and gave me her card. Damn, another accountant—the only difference was she owned her firm. I looked at the car; it was teal green, and guess what—her name was Teal. I thought that she was all that up and down. She also became someone who later did a number on me. We dated strong for about six months. She was actually thirty-four, and I was twenty-eight years old. But that did not stop me; she looked twenty-five. The first time we ever made love, she made me see stars. She said, "I could tell you haven't had it put on you like this before." I said, "No, I can't say that I have, but I am damn sure glad I am having it now." Teal made me forget about men with ease, temporarily. She was not only my lover but my friend as well. We spent our first year together attending different churches but visiting with one another's church at least once a month. The day I proposed to her, I did not have a ring nor did I sing. I did not want to curse this by going all out. After she said yes, I told her, "Now let's go get your ring." She picked out a very nice solitaire two-carat mar-quis-cut diamond. Her hands were petite, which made the rock look even larger than it was. After the engagement, she left her church and began going regularly with me. It was nice. I would buy her wonderful hats and shoes with matching bags. I never bought her any cloth-ing; she was well-versed in that area. We also complemented each other well. Too bad the engagement did not last as long as our courting period. I left town for one month on an extended business trip in New York. I also needed an opportunity to be with my family. This had to have been in mid September. I returned to Atlanta around the third week of October. Teal picked me up from the airport, and to my surprise, she had gained some weight not just in her face but also around her midsection. As we were driving to my apartment, she said that she had something to tell me. I already knew what it was; I could see the roundness of her facial features. She said, "I am pregnant." In a way, I was excited about having a child, but I did feel some sense of shame due to our being in the church and not married. When I asked her if she wanted to move our wedding date up, she said that she wanted to call the wedding off. I did not understand and was very much afraid to hear her reason; by the look on her face, she was not pleased with herself. She began to tell me that there was a possibility that the child was not mine. I could not believe what I was hearing. I asked her why she would think it was not. She spoke to me about a gentleman whom she had dated prior to meeting me. They had had intercourse a few weeks before I left to go to New York; she said the doctor told her that she was eight weeks pregnant. It could not have been mine. We had vowed not to have sex anymore until we were married, so I knew that it had been more than eight weeks since we last made love. Why me? It just seems like every time I give my love to someone, they either die or cheat; either way, they leave me heartbroken.

She placed the ring in my hand once we pulled in front of my apartment, leaned over, then held my face in her hand and kissed me on the cheek. She said, "Samuel, I don't deserve you." I got out of the car, tears rolling down my face and my heart feeling like it was under the bottom of my foot. I looked her in the eye and said, "God blessed you with me, and He cursed me with you—I just have to figure out why." I turned around and never looked back. It was not the last time that I had seen her, but it was the last time I trusted a woman. For the next year, I lived as a loner and celibate. Love and sex were the furthest things from my mind. I did, however, put more time in the church. I went to Bible study every Wednesday and church all day Sunday. If there was a program somewhere, I went. My year of isolation was actually good for me because in that time I was able to get to know me a little better. I reflected on my past, the drugs, the clubs, the men, and the women. However, the best reflection was on how God never left me. He was always there every time to pick up the pieces of my broken heart. He was more to me than anyone else in this whole world could ever be. I confided in my sister Natalie often; she was my best friend and, to this day, still is. I have always been able to share with her my most intimate secrets. This time, I needed her to help me with my next step. I was now ready to meet someone, male though. A whole year had passed, and my hormones and emotions began to find their way back into my heart and loins. A friend of mine had moved to Atlanta from New York to start a church. I did not leave my church, but I did attend his church often to help him out as much as I could. He moved here with his wife and children, but that did not stop him from opening a door that I wished he had never opened.

Pastor, Preacher, Lover, and Teacher

The Fifth Chapter

Trent was a young pastor, very attractive and very ambitious. He had three children and one very obese wife. Sometimes, I wondered if that was the sole reason for his infidelity. He and I began to hang out and go shopping for suits and ties together. I thought this was great because I saw him as a role model and someone whom I was safe with. As time went on, he began to travel out of town to preach. He asked me if I would like to begin traveling with him as his armor bearer. Basically, that is a preacher's caddy. I accepted the invitation. When I began this position, I was not a member of his church, but his members knew of me. There was one young man in particular who always seemed to give me evil looks when I attended the church for a visit or if I was armor bearing for Trent in or out of town. My guess for the constant cold shoulder from this kid was because he was attracted to Trent and I was obviously in the way. The gentleman could not have been any more than eighteen years old, but he was tall, muscular, and good-looking nevertheless. During one of my weekend excursions through Lenox Mall to find something different and unnecessary as a way to treat myself—a lonely heart will do foolish things—well, lo and behold, who was walking in my direction but the eighteen-year-old man. He nodded in my direction, so I nodded back. I walked into the Coach store, and he walked in behind me; this young man was very mature and very secure with himself. He tapped me on the shoulder and asked me if I was going to buy something for him. I once felt comfortable having older men buy me things also, so it seemed to me he may have been going down the same path I did when I was his age. I expressed to the young man that I didn't buy friends or gifts for strangers. He said that I was not a stranger as far as he was concerned. I purchased a wallet for myself, which he helped me to pick out, then I asked him if he had eaten; he said no. I offered to buy him lunch. The nervy kid had the audacity to ask if that was all he could get then he'd take it. We walked to the food court and had lunch. During lunch, he brought up my friendship with his pastor. I told him that we knew each other from New York; he expressed that so did he. I was a bit confused, seeing that he was so young. He was nineteen years old, a little older than I had assumed. He said that the role that I was doing for the pastor was what he moved to Atlanta to do. He began to tell me things that I had already been through in my life with an older person. He told me that he and Trent had been involved for over two years. That would have made him seventeen and Trent thirty-two at the time. He said that before Trent, he had never been with another male. *And the saga continues*, I thought. His name was Dontay. Dontay seemed like he really needed to talk to someone about this. I shared with him some of the things that had happened to me with Vance. It brought back memories that for over ten years I did not have to think about. He said that he was confused because he wanted to go back home and could not afford to do so. He was being supported by Trent, living in a very small efficiency kitchenette in Decatur. I asked him if he wanted me to talk to Trent about sending him home. He said that if I would help him go home, he would not have to even tell Trent; he could just leave. I felt really sorry for this young man, so I agreed to help him. I asked him how soon would he want to leave. He said he would leave tomorrow if he could. We left the mall as soon as we were done eating. He said he did not have furniture, just clothing; the place he lived was furnished and paid for weekly. I told him that he could stay at my house that evening and then we could go to the Amtrak train station the next day. It seemed like a weight was just lifted off his shoulders. We retrieved his things that were in garbage bags from the apartment. I could not see him traveling in this manner, so we purchased him some inexpensive luggage from Wal-Mart. We went to my home, where he was able to pack his things properly and securely. I contacted his mother; she and I talked for about an hour. She said that she knew that it was not going to work and that she never wanted him to leave New York. She said that because he was grown, there was nothing she could do. She had four other children younger than he and could not afford to help him, so she reluctantly let him leave. I told her that I would send him home with a few of my contacts who could help him get a job and get on the right track. She thanked me and we hung up. That night, he and I sat up and talked for several hours. I excused myself to go into the restroom. By habit, I always use the one in my room. When I came out, he was lying in my bed in his bare skin. Although this was tempting, to say the least, I could not see doing to him what was done to me and to him also already. I stayed very calm and lay down next to him, placed my hand on the side of his face. Then I softly told him that I found him very attractive and would be more than satisfied with spending an intimate moment with him but that he deserved more than a one-night stand, a long-standing true relationship. Even at a young age, I discovered the value in having a meaningful relationship with another human being. I expressed to him that I was a victim once as he was also a victim, but when do we begin to stop victimizing ourselves by placing ourselves in the same situations over and over again? You know Whitney Houston and Deborah Cox said it best, "Same script, different cast." He said that he was embarrassed but pleased that I had the level of respect for him that I displayed at that very moment. I instilled in him some of the lessons I learned from my mentors. I gave him the option to stay in contact, which he did regularly. Dontay was so much like I was, a young gentleman in his own right, just in need of a little guidance. That morning, we woke up a little late, so I called Amtrak, and a train was delayed nine hours—only Amtrak. So we ended up having the whole day together. We went down to the Underground, had lunch, and walked around. He was in desperate need of a haircut, so we did that. His haircut ended up also becoming a decent outfit to wear on the train; I did not mind. I felt that it was "pay it forward" time and that he was placed in my path for this specific reason. He said he just wanted to look nice when he got off the train. I guess wardrobe was not included in his arrangement with his pastor. I was just glad to get him out of that situation, which brewed into a heated situation for me later on with Trent, mainly because he was about to really abandon this young man after bringing him out here with no guidance or financial assistance.

I escorted Dontay on to the train with his bags and gave him his food for the trip and $250. I told him to call me whenever he needed to. We embraced, and as I held him, he leaned into my ears and said, "I could have fallen in love with you." Then he leaned back to look me directly in my eyes. I was crying, and so was he. I think I was feeling something for him as well. It's funny how that can happen. Things that you know are not good for you somehow feel like they can fill a void in your life, but you are never sure until placed in the position. In this case, I was not willing to give him a chance to prove it to me. He was only nineteen years old. Still in all, he was not your average nineteen-year-old. He had a very old and sincere heart.

Later that night, I received a very disturbing phone call from Trent. He said that he had been looking for Dontay and the woman at the rooming house described my car as the car and person that moved him out. He asked to speak with Dontay; I told him that he was gone. He expressed that I had no right to interfere, that Dontay and he had an understanding. I asked him if the understanding included an education and a way of life for his future years to come, and as I was in the heat of this discussion, I also told him that the reason I could not ever see being a member of his church is because you cannot pastor me and sleep with me at the same time. Instead of holding his own with some level of dignity, he immediately rebutted with this asinine statement: "Well, since you are not one of my members, when are you going to let me get a taste of some of that?" I told Trent that I had no respect for him and if he wanted to talk to Dontay, then he would need to speak with his mother first, since she had a few choice words for him anyway. After thirty more minutes of irrelevant debate, we ended our conversation and friendship at the same time. For the next three months, I devoted my life to a moment of seclusion. Just when I was ready to open myself back up and step out, maybe chance meeting someone interesting, male or female, cat or dog! At this point in my life, I just needed to meet someone to be close to. Also in the past three months, I had turned twenty-nine, and it was not exactly the most adventurous age, at least not for me, but around me, as usual, some form of drama was sure on schedule.

I had agreed to hang out with a couple of acquaintances and spread my wings one evening, and as I was getting pressed and primped, my phone rang. I was debating answering; for some reason, I just knew it was either them canceling with me or worse. "Hello?" "Hey,

Samuel." It was worse; it was my straight female buddy Mandalin, an older woman who was crazy as a bedbug but sweet as can be. I liked her a lot and spent a lot of time with her; however, if two weeks went by and for some freak-of-nature reason we happened to have not spoken in that time frame, her next phone call usually included a little drama, and this one was no exception. As a matter of fact, I'll just play the tape of the phone call for you:

Samuel:	Hello?
Mandalin:	Hey, Samuel.
Samuel:	Hey, Mandalin, how are you? I haven't heard your voice for a minute. What's been going on? As if I should ask. Some drama, I am sure.
Mandalin:	Well, child, you know Mother be a little busy during this time of the year. My customers like their custom-designed fashions ready for the holiday season for all those industry sets and premiers. Chile, I guess, a little extra of one's time is the price you have to pay to keep celebrities in wonderful fashions, honey. But anyway, that is not why I am calling you. Chile, I got some dirt, the kind that needs some quick cleaning. By the way happy belated birthday Christmas, baby!
Samuel:	Thanks, sweetie. No offense, Mandy sweetheart, but is this going to be a long story? I was on my way out when you called.
Mandalin:	Good, then you're dressed.
Samuel:	Hunh?
Mandalin:	Listen, you remember my girlfriend Tramaine, don't you?
Samuel:	Yes I do, how is she?
Mandalin:	Chile, her boyfriend overheard a phone conversation with her and this married man she has been seeing, and he put her behind out! She is on her way here now. She said that she is going to have to put some of her things in storage, but I told her that I would talk to you because I know that you have that extra room.

Samuel: No, sweetie, I have an office in my home. The other room is my office, capuche.

Mandalin: Listen, she is a schoolteacher, and she can pay half of those bills, giving you the other half to put yourself in more of those fine clothes I see you so greatly love.

Samuel: If anything, I would save that income, but I don't know, suppose I begin dating someone? She one of them holier-than-thou types the way she acts when you are going out to a gay club?

Mandalin: Chile, she already know you float both ways, that's why she feels comfortable with living with you. Maybe you can open her mind more to understanding your lifestyle.

Samuel: Well, tell her to call me tomorrow and . . .

Mandalin: Well, Sammy sweetie, I told her that we would come over to your house now so she could see the room. She loved the fact that you lived overlooking a lake. She needs a little calm in her life like that.

Samuel: Evidently she does not if she is messing with a married man.

Mandalin: Oh yeah! Chile, you threw me off. I ain't finished. Guess what he does for a living—he is a preacher!

Samuel: You mean to tell me the innocent churchgoing, God-fearing schoolteacher is sleeping with a married man with children, back to the Bible-preaching preacher?

Mandalin: Boy, what did I just say? Yes, dammit!

Samuel: Well, no offense, Mandy, but I am on my way out and she will just have to hang with you until tomorrow, chow.

Mandalin: Chow! Nothing, boy, please, I have a man coming over later. She can't stay here, not even a day!

Samuel: Well, she is your girlfriend! Girlfriend! So get a grip, girt up your hospitality loins, and get counseling the wounded heart, because I am in the wind. *Click!*

Henceforth, the very next day, bright and early, my phone rang, and it was Thelma and Louise. They were calling to let me know they were on their way because they had some other running around to do. I had given it a once-over and she inspected the room; she was ready to move in that night. I had given it some thought, and a little extra income for a few months did not sound half bad. I gave her a set of keys, and she gave me a check for the remainder of the month's rent. I liked her already. I would not have taken it, but that last ordeal with Dontay and Trent had set me back nearly $1,000. This to me was a good opportunity to replenish my bank account. Things were fine for the first fourteen days, then the real her came out. The novelty of her heartbreaking love breakup had worn completely off. The phone rang, so I answered it. I did not assume that she would be receiving any phone calls considering up to now, she had only received three calls from her mom. It was a male with a very distinguished voice, definitely unlike the description of her ex-boyfriend, who supposedly had a little gangster in him. I called her to the phone, and by the time she got off the phone, she was a new woman. She glided across the room like a ballerina on uppers. She yelled to me that she was going out and would probably be staying overnight out of town. Okay, not for nothing but it was 10:00 p.m., and I know she had to work the next day. I did not know her well enough, so I did not question her actions. I just decided to keep an eye on Miss Innocent Schoolteacher. About a month later, I had gone to bed around my usual, 12:00 a.m.; no more than thirty minutes later, I heard her come in. She was talking with that voice I heard on the phone. They went into her room, and within minutes, I could hear the noise of lovemaking. Forget that—it was straight-out hardcore, loud, and aggressive sex. I could not believe that this woman was this damn nasty. I had so much respect for her. Although she did sleep with a married preacher—*hmmm, I wonder if that's who is in this room*. I waited till it was nearly over and I got up and went into my living room, turned on the television, went into the kitchen, and started microwaving food; you would have thought it was 7:30 a.m. I knew they needed to wash their musky tails and were too afraid to come out of the room. The standoff took about thirty minutes before he boldly went where no man ever wanted to go. He came out first. He leaned his head into the living room with a towel wrapped around his waist. He said, "Hey, man, what's up? How you doing?" I looked up, and for a minute I was speechless; he was Samson and delightful! I said, "What's up, doc?" and immediately turned my head as though I was not moved by his presence. I was also sure that she'd already told him that her roommate was either bisexual or gay—more than likely she used the *gay* word. By my past experience, most women are often offended by men who would consider sleeping with a man and a woman. By the looks of him and the way he tried to get my attention, given the opportunity, I believe he would mess around as quickly as his next heartbeat. He was licking his lips at me as though I was next on the menu. Unfortunately I don't do dessert, nor am I ever dessert. He had the audacity to ask me for a washcloth; I got up and breezed right past him. He introduced himself and held out his hand. I sniffed his hand and then whispered in his ear, "To hold your hand and greet you as a man would be like me partaking in the sinful and disgraceful act before God you have just committed under my holy domain." He seemed to quiver at my statement, and I just could not help but laugh at his nervous reaction. He hurried into the bathroom and jumped in the shower. While he was inside bathing, I just had to get a little more scoop on Mandingo because it sounded like he was laying it down. I went into the room, and she had this tired, bashful look on her face. "Please," I told her, "honey, save it. Freaks and sluts are in the church too. You are no exception, so get over it, I did." She asked what he and I had been talking about so long. I guess she thought that we might have gotten overly acquainted with each other.

I asked her if that was the guy she got thrown out of her house for. Why I was hoping she would say no is beyond me. I just felt as though it was the same guy. She said yes, and he had two children who actually saw the two of them together one day from their school bus. That is how their mom found out and contacted her boyfriend, and that is when the doo doo hit the fan. She said, "Samuel, you are gorgeous, you can have any man or woman you want." "Look at me, I am overweight, out of shape, not pretty, and I dress funny." I told her she was the opposite of everything she just said about herself, and I was going to prove it. I told her that she was my new self-esteem booster project, and by the end of the course, she would be the true African Queen that she was. He came out and entered the room. I stood up. As I was leaving out the room, he leaned into me and said, "I did not get your name." I looked at her and said, "Tell him my name and that I don't play possum games." He was clearly bisexual. And not shy. Over the next day, she and I talked about her letting the married preacher go before it got ugly. Well, six weeks later and with very little communication on their part, ugly happened. Tramaine came home from work late one evening in tears. When I asked her what was wrong, she threw a sheet of paper on my lap that announced that she was six weeks pregnant. How crass was this, and I was in the room when she conceived! She came to me in tears because through her faith, she did not believe in abortions and knew that she could not get him to claim this child. Here I go again! Drama! For a while, though, after this ordeal, the drama seemed to fade. She was clear in her mind that she was keeping this child, with or without him. She knew that she would need to move closer to the date of childbirth, but I did get to spend the first six months of her pregnancy with her, and it was great. We walked every morning before work. She began to lose weight while she was pregnant. Her hair was growing longer, and her skin began to glow. We shopped and changed her wardrobe. She became the most beautiful, sophisticated mom-to-be I had ever seen. Sorry to say, without a husband. But she held her head up high and kept on going. We had an interesting conversation before she moved back to the town where she was from nearby. During our conversation, she asked me when I knew that I was the way I was and asked why I continued to be in the church and in this lifestyle. Had it not been for the pastor whom I had been under with the thousands of members, I would not have known how to answer her, but I had learned some things and I was equipped! I told her as he had told us, "God wants us to seek deliverance daily from the many things that we do over and over and over again. However, what makes that covenant with God solid is when we have made a conscious decision that we are turning our life over to Christ! We have already done that. But with all the things and the stuff that we bring into the house of healing that we need cleansing of, we have to know that when we stand before the Lord and ask that He delivers us, in order for it to work, we must truly in our heart want to be delivered. Now as you know, most of our sin stems from negative spirits that have taken lodge in our soul. An adverse spirit can be evicted from the temple of God. Some may lust in the sin of fornication, heterosexual or homosexual, if they like the way that sin makes them feel. But with every sin, there is consequence. This one is you get to live with all the anguish and despair, along with everything else that comes with stepping out of the will of God. God understands where we are weak, and it is that weakness that becomes our test of faith and strength in leaning to Him for our deliverance. That is one of the reasons the Bible states, 'Let everything that has breath praise the Lord.' He did not discriminate, but we do. That is why it is best for us to continue worshipping Him in the midst of our trials and storms. In a nutshell, God wants us whole, not in parts, so as we who have not been delivered from some things are still seeking God for answers, then allow us to work with Him as He is working on us. Do not judge, and do not condemn. We are all a work in progress. Selah."

After telling me how long-winded I was and how she was not in the mood for no sermon, she was, however, thankful that the Lord had spoken at that moment in the manner in which he did to both of us. Tramaine had a baby boy. She named him after me. Imagine that—his name was Chrisamuel. I sort of liked the added Chris part. She and I spoke every now and again, but of course, she found drama on the home front. *Please God!* I begged. *No more drama in my life.* So I let this newfound friend move on with her life so I could move on with mine.

Old Friends, New Drama, as the World Turns

The Sixth Chapter

Things were really going quite well. I changed jobs to a Fortune 500 company that recently expanded in Atlanta, and I purchased a downtown condo. Then all of a sudden, wham! In walks a blast from the past. I had not actually realized that a year had gone by since I had seen my good friend Miguel. I never traveled in the same circles with Miguel. He was more outgoing, hitting the clubs and the house parties and who knows what else. I was driving down Ponce De Leon from Stone Mountain, and lo and behold, standing at a bus stop was Miguel. I did not know he lived so close; it turns out that it had been the worst year of his life and he did not want to call me because he was embarrassed. If you are not careful, you can get caught up in mess in a large city, no matter where it is. He no longer lived in Dunwoody. He now lived in Clarkston, the section just north of Stone Mountain. He was rooming with a female he met in the bank. Always remember, you can't live with any and everybody, and you can't let just anybody live with you. Miguel said that he was on his way to the airport; his flight was at 7:00 p.m. It was 12:00 in the afternoon, and to drive to the airport from where I lived in Stone Mountain was just a twenty-minute drive. I told him to get in and hang out for a while; he looked stressed. He said his mom bought him a ticket and he was going to be there for two weeks to try to get cleaned up so he could return and find himself a job. I could tell that he had been getting high a lot and that he probably was out there for a minute. Boy, I would have never imagined how much. It turns out that the dude that he had fallen so in love with was a recovering crack addict when he met him. Within the third month of their relationship, he relapsed. And there begin this tale of woe. Miguel and he spent their first three months in bliss. He had a good job; Miguel was also working. Together they purchased a car, to the tune of $465 per month. Their rent was $690, but anyway, they were cozy in that Dunwoody one-bedroom. Well, Miguel wrote me a letter which he gave to me at the airport and said he was going to mail it to me; he had gotten my address from my parents in New York. We said our good-byes, and he headed home back to New York.

Ay Que Pasa Papi,

Much love to you, Sammy. I wanted to say these things to you face-to-face, but my shame and anger toward myself won't allow me to. I am about to expose enough of my past year that you would have heard enough to last you a lifetime. Anyway, that cat's name was Remy; it really was. He was smooth and cool—like me, you know, just a dude. He was sort of quiet around the house, but for some reason, he always appeared preoccupied in thought and at times even fidgety. I paid it no attention. I just figured he was trying to adjust to us living in the same household. I would say around the second month, maybe twice a week, he was calling in sick, but then he would leave the house. He told me that he would go for walks through the mall. A couple of times, I called the office, and they would tell me he left for a doctor's appointment. For one month, I sat back and observed this behavior, but it was hard to pinpoint it because he would work later the next day or he would be home when I got there, so I did not see it. This one day, I had to work late an extra four hours, so I called him at work at 10:00 a.m. to inform him of this. He said cool, he would have some dinner ready for me when I get in. He immediately told me that they were going to have a power lunch with the execs and management staff. He was a manager, so I figured okay. Then he said when they returned, they were going into a major conference that would be about three hours. If I were to do the math, this would have put him after lunch, right at the end of the day. For some reason, I just felt weird inside, and I did not call back to the office until around 3:00 p.m., hoping that maybe they had a two-hour meeting. The receptionist said that he had signed out at 11:30 a.m. I wanted to quiz her, but she and many of them at the office did not know what time it was with us, so I just stayed cool. However, I did feel like I wanted to go home for a minute to regroup and come back for the night work we had to do. I asked my supervisor if it would be okay for me to leave and come back, so could run some errands. For some strange reason, I felt inside that all hell was about to break loose, and I mean that literally, when he told me to go on and that if I needed to take an extra hour and return for just three hours, I could. I was afraid to go to the crib, but I did anyway, and you must know what I am about to tell you is very graphic and intense . . . I opened the door. Loud mellow music

was playing. It was 2:30 p.m.; the house smelled of weed and cocaine, crack cocaine! I began to get very nervous, then I heard it, the lighter. Knots started to swell in my stomach. My heart started racing. See, I HAVE BEEN IN THIS PLACE IN MY PAST, BUT I THOUGHT IT WOULD NEVER COME MY WAY OUT HERE! It's just that after this very moment, I went downhill to the point where I am now, and I JUST DON'T WANT THIS TO HAPPEN TO YOU! DAMMIT!

Well, anyway, the music was loud, so they did not hear me. I slowly cracked the door open and there it was—the scene of all scenes for the drug addict who was trying to kick this. Remy was sitting on the edge of the bed totally nude. The pipe stem was sticking out of his mouth with the lighter in the middle of his stem. I could hear it sizzle, a sound that now I wished turned my stomach instead of quenched my hunger. I pushed forward a little more to get a better view because it sounded like there were more people in the room. On the floor was another couple, male and female, and they were having sex, and there was crack next to them on the floor, and at Remy's knees, bobbin' between his legs, was some young dude no more than seventeen, and he was high! I got so pissed I blew the whole rooms high. I slammed the door! I hollered out, "If you nasty m*****f**** don't get out of my house in the next thirty seconds, I'm shootin'!" I went for my gun, Remy jumped up, booty butt naked with this nasty tweaking look on his face, talking about I needed to chill and calm down, I got it all wrong! I got it what? I told him to get out too! He had the nerve to actually step to me like he was gonna swing. I stepped back and smacked him in his jaw! Out he went! They were trying to grab drugs and whatnot. I pulled out my gun, pointed it at them, and told them if they did not walk out at that very moment with whatever they had on or off, lead pipe was the next pipe they were gonna be smoking! After they left and five minutes passed that seemed like a one-hour episode was over. I perused the room to see just what might have been sold, stolen, or whatever. Then I looked down at him, dragged him out onto the balcony, and left him lying there. He needed to cool down from that high anyway. As I began collecting the mess, I noticed that they had drugs everywhere—marijuana, powder cocaine, liquor, and crack. They were having a party in this house. I gathered all this stuff and bagged it. I wish now I would have thrown it out. That's what I told him when he came to. He tried to talk to me, but I had to ask him to leave. He said he needed a ride to a hotel. I gave him cab fare! The car was mine! He did not have much in my home, thank God. He only had some clothes and CDs. That should have told me something. Now you would think things would have calmed down for me after that. No, I needed more drama. That night, I felt like I needed to get out. Now just to let you know how far from my mind the drugs were, I was going out to get a drink, and there was plenty of liquor put away with the drugs. But the devil always seems to have a way to slide it back into your mind in order to destroy you. Anyway, I decided that I was gone go down to the club and get a drink. On Monday nights, Loretta's had a show that was usually pretty entertaining. I felt I needed one. And maybe even a hug. I went to the bar, and as soon as I sat down, it was like I had "Vulnerable Wounded Soul" written across my back. This dude came right up to me and offered to pay for my drink. He said it was because I looked so sad and I deserved to smile at least once today. Okay, that was cute! He got two points for sinking that in, but the reality was still, I did laugh once today right after my boss let me go home! That was why I was here! He began to try and put the Mack on but in a disrespectful way. Okay, I was not feeling him already! "You know what, thank you! But I will pay for my own drinks tonight as always, but you have a good evening!" But oh, how quickly the tables turned, for as I rolled my bar stool around to face the dance floor, there he was, this fine dude that always dances by himself just like I do! You know I don't like dance partners, Sammy. But then no one ever talks to me here in the ATL clubs, like no one talks to you anywhere, LOL. He took the shirt off! Okay, I was going home. Anyway, I decided after one more drink that it was time for me to get on the floor and do my thing. Somehow the crowd kind of created this opening circle that seemed to just give space to him and me as though we were in some sort of dance battle, and that whole change of area invoked just that. He and I acknowledged each other's flare and position in the room, and the battle began. He was doing stuff you never see him do. Flips, body twists, head rolls. I said, "Nah! Let's go," and the house, salsa, and calypso came spewing out. With the gyrations of my body and thrusts of my hips and torso, I could tell that he had gotten just a tad bit hot and bothered. Brother seemed like he could hold his own. After the hype drew low and he and I were sort of at that just rocking back and forth to catch your breath mode, I offered to buy him a drink. He said sure but not there. So I said, "Oh, that's cool, we could go to another club." He said, "Nah. Dude, your place if that's cool?" Then it hit me, I had a little alcohol in there. So I said, "Sure, you can follow me in your car." He said, "Nah! I'm on Marta!" Okay, cute don't always mean financially secure. So I said, well, I am off tomorrow, so if worst comes to worst, he could stay over and I would just drive him home early. Okay. Sammy, meet Cottrell, my new roommate. I know—close your mouth, I'll get to that. You know you get Jesus and it's like you can't see your feet for looking so high above the ground? You picked yourself off the floor to remember. I am not making excuses for my mistakes! Now Cottrell was real cool and calm, well-spoken, very articulate, had ambition just all over him. As we were talking and drinking our drinks, listening to the music, I could not help but reflect on what had just occurred in that very room, not even twenty-four hours prior. I needed to smoke a joint; I just gotta be real. I was feeling mighty mellow. But what I did not think about was that I did not separate the weed from the cocaine, so each of these things would be in my face. I told him that I was about to roll me a joint and that I hoped he did not mind. He said, nah! He smoked too! I said cool. Well, I pulled out the bag! And there it was—a drug addict's candy store. I pulled out the sack of weed, but something in me just wanted to taste the powder; I wasn't even thinking about the crack. I took a few bumps as I rolled the joint, and then I rolled another one. Sprinkled a little cocaine on it, and yes, I let the devil use me. And I am still paying for it. While we were smoking on the regular joint. I lit the laced one. He smelled it immediately and reached out for it. At that point, I just went back in the room and got about a gram more of powder, and we sniffed, drank, and in between, had sex. The next day, I asked him where I needed to drive him so he could go home and sleep off the rest of that wild night. He said that he was renting out a room in Decatur. I was like it never fails. I just don't attract the rich and elite like you, Samuel, do, and you don't even give them the time of day. Sammy, you get gorgeous men and women with money just offering you the world, but do you bite? Noooo! What are waiting for? I hope you ain't mad at me, Sammy! Yeah, you know I love you too! You are my homey from the home front! Anyway, I am gone make a long story short 'cause that right there is what happened. I moved this dude in—he ended up stealing stuff, selling my things, he put my gun to my head and threatened to kill me if I stopped working and paying the bills. But how could I pay bills if you are getting high with bill money? This dude was crazy. Then one day when he was not home, I found pictures of him in drag. He lived as a woman once. I mean not just for shows—you could tell from the pictures that Poppy was truly a Mommy. But anyway, I ended up getting evicted after a bunch of wild orgy parties—women and men, their friends—and now I don't even know if I might have something, you know, HIV. I am going to get

tested on Monday. While I am in New York, I'd rather be at home with my mother if I get bad news. But you know what, I still thank God because He has allowed me another day to start over. He forgave me a long time ago! So you don't have to if you choose not to. His forgiveness is enough. Peace.

Well, of course, after reading this, I could not let my closest friend come back to Atlanta from home and not get the support and help he needed, so I told him to move in with me when he returns. His mother was elated when he told her she knew that I would take care of my big brother. Although sometimes I felt like I was older. He needed to be cleaned up. There was no way I was going to let this happen to him and we not fight this demon. I struggle with sexuality. But I know when you have a crack demon among you, you have to put on the whole armor of God because Satan will use your most suppressed weakness and bring it out just when you are at the point when you can yield. This won't touch me ever again, and it did not. Anyway, while Miguel was in New York, I prepared the other room for him. I bought an extra television and extra bed; I bought calming pictures and magazines for him to read. I knew he did not have a job when he left and would probably not be able to get one right away. So I figured he could help me with some at-home administration, with my business, until . . .

WHEN LIFE ENDS AMONG FRIENDS!

THE SEVENTH CHAPTER

Ringalingaling! Ringalingaling!

Samuel: Hello?

Miguel: What's up, Sammy?

Samuel: What's up, boy? Damn, I haven't heard from you in like a month and a half! What is up, dude?

Miguel: (in a very quiet and misty voice) I got it.

Samuel: Got what, Miguel? Oh no, Miguel, please don't say you've got HIV.

Miguel: Yeah, man, I got it. Man, my whole family is up here tripping. They are crying and acting like I am already dead, yo!

Samuel: Well, you aren't, so let's keep on living. I love you, man, and I want you to know that if you have to stay in New York, I understand.

Miguel: What? Hell, no! I ain't staying here, yo! Nah! These folks would drive me crazy. I was calling to let you know I am gone need to be picked up from the airport tomorrow at 6:00 p.m. I got it for that hour because I knew you might have been done working.

Samuel: No doubt, if I had to get off early, man, it's all good. Yo! Have a safe flight. Tomorrow we'll talk, okay?

Miguel: Thanks, Sammy, I don't know what I would do if I did not have your friendship. One love, man.

Well, now I had to think about all that was about to happen. You see, after that phone call, there was more drama because although Miguel was calm on the phone, he broke down at the airport so bad I had to get someone to hold him while I went to get the car and carried him into it. When we got home, I fixed him a hot bath and a cup of herbal tea. I was gonna calm this one down real fast. He was not going to upset me no more than I already was. We talked about this, and I asked him one dumb question! How could I have been so dumb! Listen to this question: So have you told the partner you were with having unprotected sex with that you have this, and did he or you give it to the other person? He exploded on me. "Sammy! Don't you realize I could not tell you how, where, when, why, or who! Men, women, young dudes—we were out there, man! We hardly ever wore a condom. We never had enough time in between hits on the pipe before you needed another hit, man! The sex had to be spontaneous, that's what made it so wild and intense!" I told him I was sorry; I guess it had never gotten that far in my early experience. But come on, now we were in our thirties. Those were the teenage and early twenties years. Don't we gain wisdom in all things as we get older? Anyway, I did not feel I was wrong to ask. If I am your friend, then I should be able to support my friend, right?

At this point the most important thing was to find out where he stood. I asked him if I could view his test results, and I could not believe it. I asked him if the doctor had explained it to him. He said no, they had just given him the results and the numbers to some internal medicine doctors for outpatient care. I sat him down and explained to him that he was not just HIV positive but that he, in fact, had AIDS. He did not understand what a viral load was. That is why it is important for us to educate ourselves before it knocks on our door. Nor did he understand T-Cells. Miguel's viral load was 500,000, and his T-Cell count was 19. My friend was very sick and did not even know it. His loss was actually wasting from the disease. His hair thinning and darkening of his skin was not from the drugs only but also from AIDS. I took a week off from work to take him around to a few places to get him proper healthcare as well as public assistance. He was able to get food stamps, enough to pay half the bills in the house and medicine. I prepared all his meals, made his doctors' appointments, and did all that I could do. But Miguel did not want to fight the same fight. Miguel began drinking when I was at work, and I believe probably going out and getting high when he could, but he never brought it in my house. Then one spring morning, I woke up and he was hunched over the toilet, vomiting his guts out. When I looked in the toilet, I saw blood. I rushed Miguel to the emergency room. They said that he had pneumonia. They kept him. He was in there for maybe two weeks, and then quickly, sores began to grow on his body and face. He lost more weight, and I just could not understand how they could not help him. Was he that far gone? Well, one morning, it was a Saturday, around 7:00 a.m.

Ringalingaling! Ringalingaling!

Samuel: Hello.

Miguel: (*with barely any voice left*) Hey, Sammy, its Mick.

Sammy: Hey, Mick, how do you feel? You're up early.

Miguel: I never slept. I'm scared, Sammy, but I think everything is gone be all right. I mean, am I going to live, Sammy? Please tell me I am not going to die. I am not ready to die, man! Sammy, please tell me that! I think I am going to be okay because I saw an angel at my window last night.

Sammy: Oh, you did? Yeah, Mick, everything is about to be all right. (*Sniff!*) Hey, Mick?

Miguel: Yeah, Sammy?

Samuel: Do you believe that Jesus rose from the dead?

Miguel: Yes.

Samuel: Do you believe that He died on the Cross for your sins?

Miguel: Yes! Sammy, why are you asking me these questions?

Samuel: Just one more question—Do you believe that Jesus Christ is Lord and Savior of us all, born of the Virgin Mary?

Miguel: Yes, I do! Sammy, if it had not been for me watching you grow up to be who you are after all you have been through and still love God, I don't know if I could have said yes to this one. But through your walk, I can clearly say that Jesus is Lord and Savior.

Samuel: Then, Mick, you are saved. So rejoice in knowing that no matter what God's will is for your life, you belong to Him now and eternally forever.

Miguel: OK. Sammy, please don't forget to come see me today. I need you here as soon as possible, okay?

Samuel: I would not want to be anywhere else today. Hey, I'll see you in about two hours, when visiting begins.

Miguel: I love you, Sammy. Always remember that you are special, and if no one else cherishes the gift from God that you are, just know that I did. Thank you, my little-big brother, good-bye. *Click*.

Sammy: Mick, wait! What do you mean by *did*? Mick! Mick! Damn. *Click*!

Deep down, I knew what that angel that came to him last night meant he was about to leave us. I got my things together, put on some clothes and went straight to the hospital an hour before visiting hours; I just did not like how he sounded. I arrived to the hospital early to find that he had already passed on. My calling his mother after I spoke with Miguel to make plans to come here to Atlanta and meet with me was not jumping the gun. My friend had left me, and our last good-bye was a request to make it there before he went. I know in my spirit he would not have wanted to be alone. Not then. Well, I gave Miguel one of the most cherished funeral moments I could afford. His casket was ivory, his suit was ivory, and the hearse was gold with ivory curtains. I sang for his funeral at the request of his mother. It was harder than I thought it would have been. As I sang, I felt his presence in the room. All I could hear him say is, "You better sing for me, church boy." So I did.

Samuel singing:

Keep your lamps burning bright. Make a staaaaand. Stand up for what you know is right. Make Jesus first in your liiiife! And be ready whenhen Jesus comes! Oooooooooooooooooooooh! OOOOOOOOOOOOOOOOOOH! Won't you, won't you, won't you be ready, ready when Jesus comes, you've got to be ready, my Saaaavior comes, get your house, get it in order, in your life, make Jesus first, keep your lamps burning bright. Keep the love of JESUS always on your mind, and be ready, you've got to be ready, no matter what the world is doing, no matter what your friends are doing, no matter what your mothers doing, no matter what IIIIIIIIIII am doing, you've just got to be ready. Whenen, wheeeheeeee-heeeeeheeeennnnn! My Jesus commmmes!

I walked over to his mom. She held me close to her and whispered in my ear, "You just made my boy proud, and you helped him to leave this place with honor." The honor was when God opened his gates. To allow yet another soul that was given mercy, just in the nick of time, to enter into His kingdom. He is just that kind of God. Well, as for me, after that day, I decided that the only person for me right now was Jesus. I don't need anyone else. I needed Him to work on me. I hoped that I was able to enlighten some folks. And just when you feel like you're about to judge someone, do me a favor—channel that and just pray for yourself. If you don't know what to pray for, then pray for peace in their life and yours. Be good out there, and by the grace of God, be careful. I love you with the awesome love of our God.

Samuel Lampier

magazine

INSIGHT

WORLD UNITY & LOVE ISSUE

features

"STRAIGHT UP" THE HOMOSEXUAL DIGEST FOR THE STRAIGHT WORLD

CULTURE AND RACIAL DIVIDE "BEAUTY AND THE BEAST OF THE 21ST CENTURY"

ATLANTA'S BLACK GAY PRIDE "NOTHING TO BR PROUD ABOUT"

SUNDAY MORNING WHEN THE CHURCH SHOWS NO LOVE

MY VERY FIRST & VERY LAST SERMON "THE BOOK OF ROMANS SAVES US ALL"

SUNDAY MORNING
WHEN THE CHURCH SHOWS NO LOVE
ORIGINALLY FEATURED IN THE SPRING 2006 ISSUE OF *JUST LIVING MAGAZINE*, ATLANTA, GEORGIA

It was Sunday morning, and my son and I were conducting business as usual. We were getting ready for church while watching *Bobby Jones Gospel*. During breakfast, my son, then fourteen, decided that it was time for a heart-to-heart regarding our new church. We had relocated to Atlanta, Georgia, from Indianapolis, Indiana, only three months before we found what I thought was our church home. We had been attending the church seven months at this point.

Father was quite comfortable with the place of worship we'd chosen, but my son was not. He began to talk about an incident that had occurred involving himself and a young minister who was in charge of the teen ministry. He said the gentleman told him and his peers that homosexual men and lesbian women were not going to heaven. My son, though himself a straight young man, had reservations with this minister's beliefs because he was well-equipped with the Word of God. I made sure of it. I asked whether any of the other kids who had heard the minister's philosophy seemed unsure of what he wanted them to believe.

"Not after I got through with them," he said.

He told me that he let this minister and his fellow pupils know that God has salvation and deliverance for everyone, even as a person takes his or her last breath—deliverance and salvation, that is, from anything He calls sin. He told them that God does not give man that kind of authority to condemn a group of people to hell.

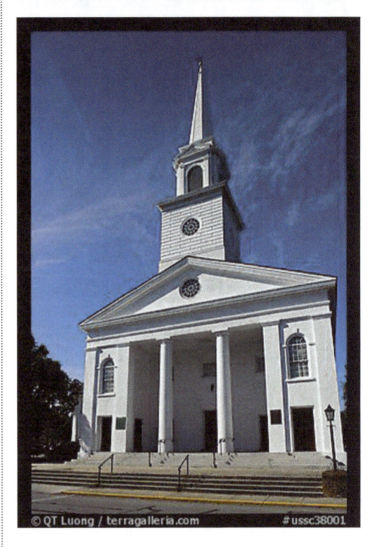

© QT Luong / terragalleria.com   #ussc38001

Let me say this, before I address this issue, that I am no stranger to the lifestyle that was the focus of his conversation. So assisting him was not my problem; being able to confront my own insecurities was. At first, I was stunned that this minister would take the subject to that level. Then I was hurt that my son felt like he had to defend his dad and his lifestyle.

Of course, our heartfelt discussion did not end there.

How could the minister say that he also wanted to know when the majority of the men were obviously gay?

"Dad, c'mon, really!" he said.

What could I say? I agreed with him on that point. What's more, I had never given our small family unit a chance to bond with this ministry before we joined. My son's continued discomfort was evidenced in that he never wanted to associate with other teens at this church. In fact, he would refuse to go to teen church and only sit with me.

I tried to volunteer as a participant with the teen ministry in order to get him involved, but several calls to the ministry leader were not returned. Then I attempted to join the choir. I auditioned, was interviewed, and was told that I would be informed of the next rehearsal to attend by mail. I never received a letter. Adding insult to injury, the leader of the choir saw me at the Sprint store, took my home and cell numbers, and told me that she had been looking for me. I never heard from her. At this point, they were stepping on my toes. How can a church tell people to get involved and then push them away? Just two weeks earlier at a very nice church func-tion they were having for the youth, I had met a couple who had joined a few months before me. She said that she was going through the same thing with the choir, but since I had not yet experienced it, I chalked it up to her not following up.

There are very few men and fathers in the church, yet pastors spend more time preaching at these men about what they are not doing than commending them on what they are doing. If he is in church to hear you speak, then begin commending him there. As I strive to raise my teenager to be a man who loves and respects the church, it's discouraging to find its leaders are making contradicting statements. They have more than enough to deal with in everyday life; pressure in the church is uncalled for.

Thankfully, we recently visited and joined a new church, and my son is now participating with the teens during service. He's even interested in joining the basketball team they have. While I'm not saying that other church is not a good church, my experience there has shown me that sometimes we need to protect our children from more than just the streets.

Written by Kevin Cavon
Author of *Church Boy in the Dark*

STRAIGHT UP!
THE HOMOSEXUAL DIGEST FOR THE STRAIGHT WORLD

This section of the book has been designed to dispel myths, rumors, and lies about the gay and lesbian culture. It also bridges the gap between the lack of understanding and a clear view of reality. Straight folk have not only condemned their own children as well as friends for being this way, but they have also alienated and cursed a whole nation worth of people who did not ask to be born that way but have overcome obstacles placed upon them in order to survive among them. We do not like the titles that were created for us. *Gay*, by definition, means "happy." This society has made us anything but that. It is now time for us to live in harmony among one another. I have been asked throughout the years many different questions from my straight friends, and I avoided most because I could not believe the level of ignorance the questions had. I no longer feel that it is ignorant of you; I feel it is remiss of us to not educate you ourselves. It does not do your soul any good to hate that which you do not understand. Open your minds. Allow the omnipotence of God to awaken you to His own children; we are no less His than you are. This digest is done in Q and A form, and it covers church and spirituality, sex and sexuality, children, parenting, and business. You will be amazed at how we are totally the same other than who we are intimately connected to.

LIFESTYLE AND LIVING

A friend came out to me. I told him that's his choice. He seemed offended. How do I handle this?

First of all, recognize that it took a lot of soul-searching before your friend came out to you like about his sexuality. It is likely that your friend is offended by your words appearing to imply that a homosexual orientation is a "choice." If your last communication was not too long ago, you could call back and apologize for your poor choice of words in saying "I respect your position," and say that you hope that you can continue to be friends. Gay people who have a history of

struggling with their sexuality are very touchy on anyone suggesting that homosexuality is a choice. He will most be likely be full of his story, wanting to tell it after having kept it inside himself for so long. All you need to do is to give him an opening, show yourself sympathetic, and be willing to listen.

Why do homosexuals think their situation is worse than that of heterosexual singles?

On first glance, the two situations would appear to be similar. But there's this big difference: Heterosexuals can always hope to meet that special someone with whom to share the rest of their lives with, even at seventy. Homosexuals are

76

tempted to despair because they see the future as one long lonely stretch, because if they accept the biblical prohibition of the Old Testament against same-gender sex and marriage, they can never hope to meet their heart's desire. Now let's get into the derogatory terms that have been equated to our humanism. Now we understand by definition, *heterosexual* is just simply the opposite word when spelled *homosexual*. However, unlike *hetero*, the abridged version, *homo*, has been used to be insulting and disgraceful.

Straight society has developed derogatory terms for gay males, especially, that have gone from generation to generation. *Queer* really means "strange." *Faggot* means "twig" or "stick." *Gay* means "happy." Unfortunately, due to our disrespect for human dignity, the word *sissy*, a nickname for sisters and several female full names such as Cecilia, has been placed in the *Webster's Dictionary* to define a feminine male. I have never been called a sissy, however. I have used the word myself, and to this day, I think about the days I have called my own that word. We have it worse, straight world, because we have not taken the time out of our busy lives to create derogatory terms for you that would be infantile. We have it worse because we are still fighting for equality in a society that is designed for your success. The media does not make mockery of your life. It is not our lifestyle, as you all suggest. It is our lives, so discontinue using the word *lifestyle* so loosely until you understand our lives. Lifestyles are chosen; life in itself, as it is handed to you, is not a choice. You have your way of life to live and accept that others have theirs.

I tried to ask this girl on a date; she said no because she did not like men. Why is it so hard to tell if someone is gay or lesbian unless they look and act like the opposite sex they are?

Well, let me set the record straight once and for all. The majority of gay males and lesbian women are as masculine and as feminine and carry themselves no differently as their siblings or parents. So you women who believe that if a man is masculine and gay he is on the DL, he is not. Most masculine gay males have never been or wanted to be with women. We don't act straight in order to not be found out; we are who we are—masculine men. Now there are those who were once masculine and years later accepted themselves as feminine. This male was probably masking what he was feeling naturally. You know him or her in school—you told him them they had feminine or masculine tendencies. Now rest assured we are not trying to deceive you; not all of us will ever be feminine men or masculine women. For the most part, we are who just who we are, so do not get angry when you are attracted to us and we are not feeling you. Or if we let you know we are gay and lesbian and your anger or hatred becomes a negative vibe toward us, for which now you look at us differently. Nooooo! Keep it real with yourself. Because you view us so differently, it kills you inside and your own self-esteem gets challenged because you realized you were attracted to a gay male or lesbian female. And you are straight! The world will continue, and you will be okay. It does not question your sexuality either; we are a very attractive community. We are very health-conscious; we love fashion, high heels, tight dresses, tight jeans, fitted tops, jewelry, and make-up. We love as well. So whether gay male or female, more than likely, you are looking at a well-maintained individual. We also maintain our youth over the ages very well. Take notes, straight people. It's fabulous to be healthy and wise!

Why are there so many gay males in Atlanta, and why are so many of them HIV positive?

Most would assume it is shallow sexual reasons that drives gay males to the city, and for a few, this may be true. However the truth is Atlanta, Georgia, over the years has become the home of the CDC (Center for Disease Control). There is a benefit of being in a city where there are numerous public and private centers for infectious diseases. Medications are tested here and are given at discounted to no costs for those who do not have health insurance. AID Atlanta, one of the largest wellness facilities in Atlanta, has done tremendous nonprofit work in this city and should be praised for its existence. They offer free screening, care coordinating, and healthcare, and there is Absolute Care Medical Center, which has doctors on sight and a pharmacy. They care for a large number of straight men and women as well as gay males with HIV/AIDS. The lesbian community is very fortunate that this disease has not hit their community because they do not have sex with men. But the straight females, especially in the African American community, need to be aware that it is important to protect yourself, and before you decide to have intercourse with your mate unprotected, have them tested with yourself. The results come back in minutes, just the same amount of time it would take to contract the disease. You can find out that you nor does your mate have it. Also we are able to prosper greatly here; that is the greater reason. We are successful entrepreneurs. We have six-figure to million-dollar homes, and we are able to do this under minimal stress. Now to answer the last part of the question: so many of us are HIV/AIDS infected because of immaturity, denial, or ignorance of the facts. Many gay males believe that once they have been diagnosed, they cannot be reinfected with the virus, and that is far from true. Each person carries a different strand of the virus. Each time you have unprotected sex, you risk the chance of making it harder to treat your virus. I do apologize for those in our community who indulge in risky sexual behavior. I pray they one day get it before they end up young and on an obituary. We are losing a lot of young members of our community.

Why do fewer gay and lesbian people have long-lasting relationships than straight people?

Not every gay relationship is short. Actually, most lesbian relationships last over five years or more. The ones that are, are short for the same reasons straight relationships are. Being gay isn't just about sex, contrary to popular belief. When you are gay, you want a truly meaningful relationship with the same sex for the emotional bond that we feel toward the same sex naturally. Granted, homosexual and heterosexual people can just want sex instead of a full-blown relationship. There isn't a difference in how long gay relationships last versus straight relationships. The one thing that I will say is different that bonds couples who are straight for twenty years or more are children. When you create a child, that adds to the marital bond, or at least it is supposed to. Raising or committing to raising children locks that couple in easily for the next eighteen years to one another if they consider their children. That's why many straight men leave their wives after the children are gone. He was never there for the marriage. And if anyone says differently, I will let you know that they have no scientific basis for their opinions. Isn't it a fact that two-thirds of heterosexual marriages end in divorce?

Technically, the last statistics taken show divorce rates closer to 34 percent; only when you double that number to accommodate for other nationalities does the number skyrocket, which is a common mistake, but that's not the point. The point is that some gay relationships do not last as long due to the same reasons as straight relationships, but with the added fact that in some countries, homosexuality is treated like a plague, and the religious leaders condemn that life. This, of course, is heard on the highest levels of government, and before you know it, there are laws passed to prevent homosexual marriages. The other end of the equation is that when that way of life is not so widely accepted, there is tension between the partners due to the fact that some people do not want to tell their friends or families. It very much falls to a situation in which you are ashamed of your lover. Eventually they see this and leave. Until people from all walks of life are fully accepted in our societies, the statistics will be unfavorably skewed.

I was at LA Fitness and saw dudes showing their privates in the sauna. Why have gay males made the gym another pickup place?

That is something I unfortunately have to admit to be true but also something that I also left the gym for. I would like to address this but direct it to those who participate in these behaviors. You do not know who is gay, straight, or crazy in these places. Many persons have lost their lives for disrespecting someone; it is sexual deviancy. I may be like you, but that does not mean I want to be accosted by you. I am not a person that takes kindly to being propositioned or flashed in the gym. I have reported guys who touched me or showed me their private area intentionally. It is perverse and places you at a degraded gutter level. Please stop making our community seem like all we do is meet each other and have sex. Also have some class and respect for yourself. When I was younger and wanting be out there getting high and being promiscuous, I always stopped and said, "I am my mother and father's son, and this is who I say she is by representation when I walk out my door." And I do look at people and determine what type of upbringing they must have had based on their level of character. Usually those gay males, who are always seeking instant gratification by having one-night sexual encounters, are not used to daily love and affection growing up from family or friends. It should not be a comfortable thing to feel it is okay to seduce, stare at, or step to another man if he has not given you any indication that he is interested or think that because he is in the gym in a tight bottom or top that he is gay. This goes for lesbians as well. Respect our straight brothers and sisters in these places that we share intimate areas like locker rooms, saunas, and showers.

Why do gays and lesbians believe they are born that way?

We do not think it! We know it! Most of us realize this from early childhood as soon as we begin to feel and realize our sexual self shows no intimate attraction to the opposite sex. However, you will find that a male child in his toddler years feeling more comfortable playing with a group of girls than standing around with other little boys, plotting on the girl he is fond of. Just like the tomboy female may prefer to play basketball during recess or wrestle with the guys. She and he are only doing what comes to them naturally. Their DNA produces a masculine or feminine trait that causes their comfort level to be that of a person who is straight and desires to do the same things naturally. As this toddler enters teenage years, as with straight people, your sexual desires intensify and you become attracted to a certain type of opposite sex. The same holds true in the gay and lesbian society; we are not attracted to one another just because we like the same sex. Nor are we attracted to you automatically because you are straight. We too have preferences of personalities, physical traits, and even astrological birth sign compatibility. I go into this in more detail in the sermon portion. We need to relate this to a God creation and not a man creation through

His Word. Adam and Eve had more to do with this than we care to admit or believe.

Why do gays and lesbians not feel they are mistakes or freaks of nature?

- If God felt that we were such, He would not allow us to be rulers over much! And we do so with taking downtown city streets of major cities and developing upscale living and businesses for ourselves, in which we open our doors to all.
- We raise children for which you fight against us, having become successful products of society. Many of us are raising children that are our own, or acting as parents of nieces and nephews. We adopt as well. The difference is because we give these children a greater understanding of loving people unconditionally, they become successful in everything they do. You don't find too many of us on the court shows or in the courtrooms with our children.
- Because God blesses us so much and those of us who serve Him and seek Him, He speaks to us in a voice in which He proves His ways and thoughts are far beyond ours. However, those of us who do not serve Him and live out of His will not because of their sexuality but because of their sins, they do perish.

GAYS AND LESBIANS IN THE CHURCH AND SPIRITUALITY

Why are there so many gay men in the church?

Well, let's first acknowledge that they are men first, and then the answer will become so much clearer in its point. Now understand God can use and will use whomever. Believe it or not, gays and lesbians are called to ministry by God. More than you are probably willing to accept right now because if I began to not expose but reveal to you some of your noted persons in ministry who are even only married because of our society but unfortunately are condemning themselves as they preach and pour into us, many of you would be distraught and will leave the church. Now here is where we come into play. We are the persons they come to for comfort, solace, and yes, romance. Now here is how we take each other down. Can you guess how many commandments were broken just in this one love triangle? Not all of these relationships are sexual because a man or woman of God suppresses what's inside them to maintain their status, their home, and their ministry I commend. No different than the celibacy of a priest or nun. They seek friendships with us in order to have the psychological balance restored because our way of life is not about the sex. It is about our love and affection of one another. They don't lose the desire for sexual relations with the same sex; they just abstain.

God gives us the same blessings for our tithes that you get. We live just as well and, sometimes, better than others, God provides us with jobs and businesses that you see us at every day. And God uses us to teach love unconditionally because in spite of the hate that is thrown at us in church and in the media and in the streets, we continue to go to church, we continue to love God, and we continue to participate in ministry, and that is our way of fighting against the enemy that has become you. So yes, when you see us in church, it's because you can't stop us. It belongs to God.

Isn't homosexuality a spirit like deception?

Okay, I know a lot of pastors and preachers are not going to be happy about this, but whatever. God has already said He is the spirit that dwells in us. So at what point do the character defects that derive from our upbringing, peers, and wrong choices have anything to do with the only Holy Spirit that dwells in us, in which no other spirit can dwell in your body with God? If you deceive people, lie, cheat, steal, or kill, you have sinned before God's commandments. You will not be able to cast out the spirit of homosexuality because you cannot cast out the spirit of heterosexuality because they are not spirits! Selah (think on these things).

Why do gay _and_ lesbian people feel it's necessary to display their orientation in church?

Where were you when this happened? Most gays and lesbians don't unless we are questioned or confronted or are overly feminine or masculine. Coming out as ourselves especially in the church will help others to see that gays and lesbians are ordinary people who love Jesus as much as they do, and it will enable them to be more kind and "enlightened" in their relations with other gay people. It really hurts our community when the people who sit beside us in the pews make rude remarks about homosexuals. You are this devoted Christian who loves God but have no love for your brother or sister, yet you are supposed to be living and displaying a Christ-like image. I am confused about something. Where in the Bible did God say it was okay for anyone to ostracize or single out someone else for who or what they are? The days of stoning are over, at least in our culture, so what are you expecting

to happen? When we are the topic of a sermon, nothing happens. We don't change because thus saith you. It's necessary so we can live in peace that we understand God is who is in our individual lives before He is with us collectively in church. Don't preach to me about who I am if you don't know who I am in God.

GAYS AND LESBIANS RAISING CHILDREN

Part 1. Won't a child turn out gay or lesbian if they are raised to view same sex as a healthy relationship?

Although in our world this is a joke to us of the thinking of straight people, we are trying to figure out how we can adjust our lives to save the ones you all put in foster care. And we get a fight often for that. It is only based on your own ignorance and incompetency to seek knowledge. Our children are raised with the same or better values that we were raised under. For some of us, as also with you, children changed those of us who may have been on destructive paths and made us more responsible. A child seeing two females who love each other but inside knows she is straight herself is raised by us to understand the opposite sex. We prepare our children for dating as well as understanding sex with the opposite sex. Now the only advantage of a child who may be gay is, this child will not be rejected by us but safely guided through this way of life because we have to protect this child with greater care from society's hate.

Part 2. Can a Child Become Gay Living with a Gay Parent?

No! And I am speaking from example. I raised my son on my own. He understood my

81

sexuality by age eleven when I confirmed it with him. He has lived with myself and partners, and our partners, especially those who were raised in similar households, make great balance factors in our children's lives, like a stepparent. My son has dabbled in street gangs, stealing, and lying; however, today, I am proud to say my son is in the Army, Airborne, and doing extremely well. He is still under twenty-one years of age and already has been to college for culinary arts, which he did at age sixteen. He discusses with me his desire to one day be a father as well as find the type of woman I find acceptable for him. We are excellent parents; my son told me he would not want to have had a straight dad after having been able to compare his friends' dads to me. He realized he had the nurturing love that a mom can give and the stern discipline and security that a father gives. His friends, those who even know their straight dads, are hardly ever told daily as I tell my son whenever we talk, "I love you, son or daughter." Men tend to be so macho, especially with their sons. When he is young, he does not need your machismo; he needs your love, your hugs, your words of encouragement. Your praise when they are doing well. Fathers need to rise up, period. It's not about the black father; it's all races who have declined in fatherhood and family values. What were you doing at age eighteen, my straight brothers? Let me tell you what I was doing. I was working on Wall Street, going to college, and I had taken in a fifteen-year-old former high school track buddy and freshman brother. His parents could no longer afford the private school we both attended, so since I had a job, I told him to stay at my home with my family. My mom made me treat him as though he were my son. I had to make sure he had all his school needs. I saw him through a track scholarship to Pittsburgh State University, and he is a productive man today. Then I had my own son and raised him by himself. That is being a man,

being a father. Yet we have all these women saying they want a real man. First define him, and then seek him. You say you want a real man, then you go get a thug who whips on you and make you pay his bills. But he has great sex. That's a real man? Do you need another example? Okay, two weeks over the summer of 2009, my partner and I had two of his nephews with us. They understood our relationship at ages eleven and thirteen and had no problems with it. However, they had concerns about girls and sex, they had issues with school, and the eleven-year-old was more advanced in his walk with Christ than the thirteen-year-old. They both needed men to talk to. They were not brothers but cousins. By the time they left us, they had clear understanding of why it is important to wait until you are older and mature to handle sex, so to abstain now would be important for their personal success. They both had to revere and worship God on the Sundays they were with us. They were both having challenges in school. Well, I recently got a report from the thirteen-year-old that he is now saved; he has gone from a D and F student to four As, two Bs, and one C. Parenting is more than producing a child and watching them grow. It is daily nurturing and instructing. We fault our young people today for being wild and ruthless, yet we ignore their cries for attention, love, understanding, and teaching them commitment to their responsibility. *Fathers!* Blacks, Asians, whites, and now we have influenced the most family-oriented race, the Hispanics, where traditionally the father would die before he left his family. America, kudos on your great efforts in showing other countries how to destroy the family! *We might as well go ahead and take credit for it.*

The last thing any of you should ever go off about us raising children is us raising children. So many children have been forced into foster care by so many of you! The last thing you all need to do is complain about us having children, adopting children, or even fostering children, because you all are the ones that are causing them to be without parents. Straight folk! Get on the radio and talk about that! Ask some parents who gave their children up, why and what are they doing with their lives now that is so positive for that decision to have been made? I am asking you all really to do this. Restore the family. You all have missed the focus. Again, straight folk, you have allowed the media to shift us from what's really important. How about working toward getting the thousands of African American children who will not be adopted because of their race and find themselves on the streets after emancipation? I am willing to work with all you radio and talk show hosts to open up this discussion so we can restore some homes and many children's lives. In order to restore the sanctity and strength of the family unit again, we must reconnect and make each member a valuable asset to the continuance of our generation and legacy. Cutting off a member of the family is like breaking off a branch from a tree and allowing it to just wither away with no real connection to anything else ever again.

How does a child know that they are gay or lesbian?

It is as natural an emotion or feeling as you have as a heterosexual, although children learn early the dislike for the feeling of attraction of the same sex due to the influence of boy meets girl. He or she most times will suppress an emotion if society is not teaching them on how to respond to those feelings. A child that is too soft for a male or too masculine for a female is either beaten, yelled at, disliked by either or both parents, or made to dress in manners which do not please them. So this child learns to watch or befriend the other children whom they can tell like the opposite sex and begin to mimic the behavior in order to be

safe in the places that the child has to frequent every day like home and school.

When a heterosexual child comes home at six years old and says, "Mommy, I have a boyfriend," we are pleased that at such an early age we can identify their sexual preference. Normally the homosexual child will learn to mimic the straight child in order to gratify your wishes. As the child gets older, he or she will seem rebellious. But it is not rebellion; they have now learned to make themselves happy and accept who they are in spite of your beliefs, your dreams for them, or your blessings. This child that you think has just made a decision to be gay has really just made the decision to not care what you think; it is not your happiness as an adult they seek. Children want so much to please their parents; they will do whatever it takes to make us happy, even play sports they can't stand. But now you have an adult who has always known who they are. Understand this if you feel that your small child may be gay or lesbian. Don't force them to do things they are not comfortable with; you will create an insecure person. Understand first that he or she is a person; mold them to believe in them. Learn what he or she likes in fashion, and if it is too feminine or too masculine for a boy or girl, figure out ways to compromise the look instead of saying no. Children today are more aware of who they are than we were because the media exposure and Internet gives them access to answers to questions we won't answer. So we can't bluff, force, or control these minds; the only thing we can be is the greater influence. And that takes patience, understanding, and acceptance.

Don't homosexuals seduce children?

There's no real evidence that homosexuals seduce proportionately more children than heterosexuals. Those who are sexually attracted to children are called pedophiles, and they may appear to be heterosexual, homosexual, or bisexual. Gay people are attracted to sexually mature people of the same gender. Pedophiles are attracted to prepuberty children of the same, the opposite, or either gender. Pedophiles, who are most often male, may exhibit a preference for boys, but that is not the same as a homosexual orientation. It appears that most child sexual abuse is perpetrated by fathers, stepfathers, mothers' boyfriends, uncles, brothers, or close family friends; almost all are found to be heterosexual.

My son has a gay friend. Does this mean he wants my son to be gay?

No, it does not. My son is straight. I raised him to respect all people. Just because someone is gay does not mean that God did not send them to your life. Be careful of your son's friends whether they are straight, gay, or lesbian; all children are susceptible to peer pressure. There are more influences out there for your child that you should be more concerned about. My son has a gay friend whom I have the utmost respect for. I trust him around my son, and my son is secure with him and is grateful for their friendship. He knows my son is straight, so he does not involve him in all aspects of his life. My son had gang-affiliated friends once, which nearly cost him his life. Which would you prefer?

THE POLITICAL DIVIDE

Why do gays need special rights?

Our community has never asked for special rights. We have only asked for the same provisions that are afforded to the straight community, such as health insurance for our spouses and tax breaks for co-homeowners. The media has a way of blowing topics well out of proportion. We are victims, fools, and slaves of false dialogue from the media.

OUR RECENT HISTORY

The Late Harvey Milk

Gay men and lesbians were coming out in droves all across the country in the late 1970s. In response, a legislative political attack aimed at gays and lesbians was mounted by California State Senator John Briggs, who introduced Proposition 6 onto the state ballot. The measure was intended to ban all openly gay persons from working in the public school system, for fear they might be perceived as role models. For the first time anywhere in America, gay issues were being played out in the political arena. Rob's original idea was to make a film about this campaign and the issues and conflicts the situation presented.

Harvey Milk emerged as the leader in the fight against Proposition 6. Harvey Milk had only recently been elected to the San Francisco Board of Supervisors, making him the first openly gay politician in California to be elected to office. Tirelessly campaigning throughout the state, Milk debated Briggs on the issue, revealing his wit, humor, anger, and charisma to a much larger public than ever before. On the first Tuesday of November 1978, Proposition 6 went down to a resounding defeat. Just weeks later, on November 27,

1978, Harvey Milk was murdered in his city hall office, as was Mayor George Moscone, by disgruntled former supervisor and police officer Dan White.

Standing on the front steps of San Francisco's City Hall along with other San Franciscans immediately after the assassination and marching were fifty thousand San Franciscans walking with candles silently down Market Street that evening. The story didn't end with the Proposition 6 campaign; that was only one manifestation of anti-gay beliefs that were being brought to surface as gay men and women found their rightful place. Harvey Milk's murder was another.

On May 21, 1978, the Dan White trial concluded with White receiving a minimum seven-year sentence for "involuntary manslaughter." Riots broke out in front of City Hall, where a dozen police cars were torched. In 1986, after being released from prison with time off for good behavior, Dan White committed suicide in his home. Aimless and depressed at failing to put his life back together after serving an absurdly short five-year prison sentence for the double murder (he was actually convicted of manslaughter instead of murder?), White died knowing he had elevated his nemesis Harvey Milk to iconic martyr status, which probably gnawed constantly at his vitals during the seven years he survived his victim. Harvey would undoubtedly have preferred a longer life than the fifty years he was given, but he had been fatalistic about the likely price he would pay for his open political activism. Milk tape-recorded a manifesto to be played in the event of his murder, so he was as prepared as one can be for the eventuality that overtook him on November 27, 1978.

Why is "Don't ask, don't tell" so important?

"Don't ask, don't tell" is a form of discrimination because once a person does ask and when we do tell, in the military, it has damaging effects. Unfortunately, to a vast number of people, our lives are not taken seriously. It has caused many of us to lose our rank, gain dishonorable discharges, and be ridiculed as well as not promoted. If we are allowed to fight incognito and still do the same level of work as the next man or woman, then knowing who we are in places you are not, our bedroom, should not matter. What you do in your bedroom does not cost you your careers and livelihoods, straight people. And think about the amount of infidelity and explicit sex that goes on behind your doors.

Listen, we do not concern ourselves with your life behind closed doors, so why are you so concerned about our life behind closed doors? Our government may as will be a dictatorship as far as how I have seen it operate on matters concerning this nation's citizens; we have become now third-class citizens to those who are straight. We ask for things that are simple human dignified rights, and they have to go through congress, be turned into bills, and then what? Will people automatically change their mind-set because a bill was passed to treat us better? No, that is only going to come from understanding that we are as human as you are.

So if you are allowed to get married, does that mean you want to have a big church wedding too?

If I were to say no, we would not like that, I would be wrong; again, we are just like you. Some of us are elaborate and wealthy enough to have that, and some of us are modest and prefer simple and economical. As far as the church thing, preachers and pastors, you all can stay out of Washington, DC. Our desire is not to come down your aisles. If you have not noticed, in most states and many cities, we have our own churches that welcome us, and those who do that are not alternative; they make themselves known through our publications. We also prefer to not be placed in uncomfortable positions just to do what you do in your ceremony and that is to have God recognize our union. We are only being obedient to the Word of God by doing this, as it states in 1 Corinthians:

> Now to the unmarried and the widows I say: It is good for them to stay unmarried, as I am. But if they cannot control themselves, they should marry, for it is better to marry than to burn with passion. (1 Corinthians 7–8)

"The Book of Romans Saves Us All Sermon" awaits you . . .

I was in my apartment leasing office, and this gay couple was refused tenancy even though they qualified. Do apartment complexes have that right?

All home managements reserve the right to not approve tenancy for whatever reasons, but discrimination of sexual orientation is not allowed. In Atlanta, many private renters will not lease to two gay males or two gay females. Their reasons range from parties to their discomfort of seeing two like individuals in love. Unfortunately, this comes from another ignorant place. Now if you look at places like Atlanta, Chicago, Indianapolis, Los Angeles, New York, San Francisco, and many more, they all have this in common: a striving, affluent, and upscale gay community. We have developed in these downtown cities million-dollar high-risers, ¼ of a million-plus-dollar town

homes, apartments and condos, restaurants, and stores. A large number of us pay greatly into our taxation because we own as much as you do. Personally, the majority of my friends who are gay or lesbian are doing it! Big! So continue to discriminate, Ms. Leasing Agent. When you turn us away, God opens a better door each and every time. So we thank you. Keep up the good work!

THE SEXUAL ASPECT

Why do lesbian women use a strap-on (faux penis) and still not want to have sex with men?

First, you must understand that not all lesbian women have the desire to have penetration. Often, the stud partner (masculine lesbian) feels no different sexually than the straight male. Her female organ is in her mind for one purpose only. For urination, most often she only desires to give oral sex and not receive. The fem (feminine lesbian) will feel sexually most like a straight female; thus her natural emotional attraction is to still be with the same sex. As with some heterosexual males who desire from their female partner certain things that can make a man appear to have some homosexual sexual tendencies, i.e., having his nipples licked or the desire to have anal intercourse with the female, the female who allows herself to be have intercourse with another female using a strap-on is still very secure with her sexuality. She is not confused. She still would prefer a softer skin next to hers, definitely not razor stubble. That's a turn-off to her, just naturally, no matter how fine she is.

Aren't gay men and women attracted to all other men and women?

LOL at this one! My straight brothers and sisters, don't you have a preference? Then that answers this question. I have been in places where guys acted like I touched them by their body language; the funny thing is they noticed me before I can even acknowledge their presence. I am not attracted to thugs, saggers, and guys with no jobs, no car, and those whose names do not appear on a deed or lease. He has to have some sense of class and dignity, no matter his upbringing. And he has to be an example to my son, or he does not get past the initial conversation. We level ourselves just like you. We validate who we are and our worth, and we select partners based on that. Some of us are like you; we are wonderful inside and out and don't realize it, so we settle for less than our worth. We do it too. I have done it often since I have lived here in Atlanta. But more than likely if you are straight and we know it. Even if we are attracted to you, and we are being mature, then we will never cross a boundary that will make you uncomfortable or confrontational. There is a comfort in not having to deal with rejection. We do that to each other enough in our community we don't need any outside help.

Do gays and lesbians role-play in order to have a male and female image?

That is a myth that we must end here. We do not role-play. We do not have to because we are who we are sexually, naturally. Once we have accepted our sexuality, our initial sexual experiences usually define our preference. I guess the best illustration would be in the gay male world; we have classifications that identify who we are sexually.

- **Top**—He is more likely to be a masculine male, but not necessarily. He does not like to be penetrated, nor does he like to give oral sex (does not always apply). His relationship and sexual preferences would be a bottom male, versatile male, versatile top male, or a versatile bottom male. Either way he is doing the penetration. He would be the closest example of the straight male in our community. Top men tend to be selfish sexually; however, there are many who dabble occasionally on the bottom end. They call it "feeling that way for the moment."

- **Bottom**—He is more likely to be a feminine male, but not necessarily. He only wants to be penetrated and does not like to penetrate other men. He likes to give oral sex but does not care too much for it to be done to him. He is more comfortable with an aggressive top male; a versatile top would work for him, only if he has no desire to be penetrated during their relationship.

- **Versatile top**—He is more likely to be a masculine male but not necessarily. He does not mind being penetrated occasionally but much prefers doing the penetration. His relationship and sexual preferences change somewhat from a top. He would be sexual with a bottom male but would not feel 100 percent complete in a relationship with a bottom male. He is more comfortable in a relationship with a versatile male, a versatile top male, or a versatile bottom (his ideal match).

- **Versatile bottom**—He is more likely to be either masculine or feminine. he prefers to be penetrated in bed but will occasionally penetrate another male, mainly his partner. Relationships for him are best with a versatile top male, a top male, or a versatile male.

- **Versatile**—He is, of all, the most flexible sexually and can be with almost anyone sexually. However, in relationships, he is not comfortable with a total top male. He is best suited in relationship with either a versatile top or a versatile male such as himself. He is equally in tune with his sexual preference; he likes to give and to receive on almost all aspects sexually.

- **DL**—He is our newest oldest addition. Because he has always been on the scene, it's not until HIV/AIDS that he has come to the surface. His desires range from many because most often, he comes to this lifestyle seeking that which his wife or girlfriend won't do and then some things women don't do with men that men do with each other orally, anally, and in foreplay, in which men understand each other's body and what it needs.

Are bisexual people just confused about what they want?

Yes and no. Many bisexual people are your closet cases or your DL male or female; however, here is the kicker. In order to be bisexual, you have to be homosexual in your natural sexual instinct. Like with a black male impregnating another race, the dominant gene is always the black gene. Same difference—the dominate gene for a bisexual individual is that of a homosexual. Many bisexual people will admit that they enjoy same sex intercourse over the opposite sexual intercourse. Then again, many won't admit it, at least not to their straight relations.

Does it mean that I am gay because I like to watch two women have sex? It just seems more acceptable to me than two men.

No, it does not mean you are gay, but it does speak to your homosexual tendency, although it is displaced with your straight attraction toward women. To desire or be intrigued by the homosexual sexual activity of two women does have to do with your own homosexual inhibitions. This is not a scientific fact. But it does not take science to understand human nature. If it sickens you to watch two men but quenches your thirst to watch two women, you are already desensitizing yourself to same-sex intercourse in itself. After watching so much of that, you eventually become numb, and if by chance a scene comes up where two men are involved, you will be less likely to fast-forward or skip to the next frame. You are human, and we are curious beings; much goes on in our minds that no one will ever know. I had a straight friend tell me that I was so beautiful inside and out that if he were gay, he would snatch me up off the market. That did not make him gay, but he identified with his feminine side to actually define what he would be attracted to if he were gay. Most straight men can do that, like when Maxwell was in his prime, I heard many guys say, "Man, if I were gay, Maxwell would be the one." They were mesmerized by his vocals and his swooning nature that gets into anyone's soul. And he was and is a very sexy black man. Many of you admire us from afar, and it's cool—we can be friends. It won't make you gay, nor would watching two women, unless you are not careful. By the way, I do not condone porn or any explicit sexual behavior, just for the record.

THE CANDID PERSPECTIVE

Let's be candid, those of you who say you find homosexuality offensive. What is it that offends you? Unless you come into our bedrooms and observe us being intimate, what the hell are you offended about? We don't try to imagine what you do behind closed doors; some of the things you may do sexually would

offend your mother or father to know how uninhibited you really are. So clean out your own house. The media and the newspapers have exposed so many pastors and preachers this season for what they are doing behind closed doors. Stop deflecting your inadequacies by bringing out the negative that you consider in others. Straight people need gay people to make themselves look better, from my perspective and that of so many of us. You all have corrupted society with your ignorant, biased, prejudiced, hateful, ineffective opinions of others. Evaluate yourself first. The one good thing I can say about those who are gay and lesbian: other than having to deal with simple, straight folks, we are the most secure "with who we are," our selves walking the planet. It is your own insecurity, straight people, that has you bound and so wrapped into our lives you cannot fix the mess that is yours. We are birthed out of the sperm cells and wombs of straight people.

Take a survey, answer these questions, and who you are and how you think may surprise you.

1. Why does it matter to you so much whether a person is gay or not?

   _____
   _____
   _____
   _____

2. Why do you feel it is okay to talk about or look down on a person if you find out that they are HIV positive or have AIDS?

   _____
   _____
   _____
   _____

3. Why do so many of you come to us and are our friends when no one else is around but act like we just met when others show up?

   _____
   _____
   _____
   _____

4. Why do you care whether we marry or not?

   _____
   _____
   _____
   _____

5. What did a gay or lesbian person ever do to you to make your life miserable?

   _____
   _____
   _____
   _____

6. What have you ever done to a gay or lesbian person to make their life miserable?

   _____
   _____
   _____
   _____

7. If your child told you they were gay or lesbian, how would you handle it?

   _____
   _____
   _____
   _____

8. Do you think it is okay to single out another man's life that he was born into and call it a choice they made?

9. When did you wake up and choose to be a heterosexual?

_____

_____

_____

_____

10. If it is a choice, I dare you tomorrow to wake up and say, "I choose to be gay today," then write down all of the natural gay and lesbian tendencies that arise immediately. If none arise, then guess what: you cannot make a choice. Stop the ignorance!

_____

_____

_____

_____

I just have this to say in closing: if your mother, father, sister, brother, son, daughter, uncle, nephew, niece, or aunt opens their heart to you and tell you that they are not straight, first understand that they are also dealing with acceptance of themselves; your nonacceptance brings to them an unnecessary shame for something they have no control over. Many of us wish we were born straight, including me. We cry ourselves to sleep, pray that God removes it from us, and listen to pastors who tell us to come to the altar for them to lay hands on us and remove it. Guess what, it never works! And those who said it did, I bet a dime on the dollar they are not telling the total truth. Abstinence does not equate permanent removal. I love all people, even those who try to harm us, because God said so. Do I always feel the same love in return? No, of course not. But I don't have to receive it in order to know how to give it. I love with the love of God. If you can look back and say that you mistreated someone because of their sexual and not spiritual orientation, then you still have time to ask God for forgiveness and never repeat it.

CULTURE AND RACIAL DIVIDE
BEAUTY AND THE BEAST OF THE TWENTY-FIRST CENTURY
(ORIGINALLY FEATURED IN THE JUNE 2003 ISSUE OF METRO CIRCLE MAGAZINE, INDIANAPOLIS, INDIANA)

Growing up in the city of New York, a child can be exposed to many different things. Some of these things, a child coming of age should never experience. However, there were life experiences that other children from smaller cities should have been so blessed to see. The experience I cherish the most was the amazing vast diversity in the culture within New York City. When my family lived in the South Bronx, one of New York City's large boroughs, we saw a tremendous amount of cultural diversity within our neighborhood. Due to low income, the majority of our neighbors were either Hispanic or African American. My family and I lived among Hispanics from Cuba, Puerto Rico, Honduras, the Dominican Republic, Belize, Panama, Spain, and Mexico, and that is just to name a few. We also lived among Caribbeans from many islands.

Although our neighborhood was categorized into two ethnic groups, as I became friends with many in the area, I learned that there were many cultural differences within each ethnic group. Not only was this experience invigorating, but it was also an excellent social learning tool that helped me to understand the realities of life, which I will hold on to forever. Gaining a respect for our cultural differences and even more respect for our cultural similarities is something one receives during their growth process while living in New York City. By the time I was a teenager, my family moved up in "class" and relocated to the North Bronx, where the more affluent individuals lived who still wanted to live on the Bronx but desired a lifestyle of the suburbs. Only this time, things changed a little for us. Our neighbors, not only on our street but on other streets as well, were Irish, Italian, Hispanic, Indian, and African American, and of African or Caribbean descent. We could not choose if we wanted to live in a predominantly black or white neighborhood because it did not exist.

I expressed all this to say, "As beautiful a thing as culture is supposed to be to our individual beings, we have made the individuality of race a disgrace, not only on this earth but also before the eyes of God. We have criticized each other based on what other races eat, how they dress, the music they create and listen to, and even the homes they build to live in. Moving to the city of Indianapolis, Indiana, in 1998 surprisingly took me back in time to a period that I had only read about in history books, where self-pride and pride of my own culture did not exist due to the emergence of slavery and segregation. I have witnessed more self-hate and cultural divide than I had ever believed to still be a part of this world, where the Ku Klux Klan are still allowed to hold annual protests downtown. I am not putting the city down for it is a beautiful city, but when it comes to race, there is "the Beast." It is the ugly ogre that rips through the heart of this precious city. You may not believe this, but a metropolitan city cannot survive on hate forever. It is illogical to believe that one can. Hate causes segregation, riotous behavior, frustration, and anger within our communities for little to no reason at all, for example, because I moved into your neighborhood you do not like me. OK, you

have just caused yourself a mound of stress, and I may turn out to be the best neighbor you have ever had in your entire life. In three words, "Get over it!" Everyone has the right to prosper in this city as well as to live where they economically can afford to live, shop where they choose to shop, and ask for the sake of God, worship where you want to worship.

Let us embrace each other's culture for it is not difficult to do but rather easier to become more aware and to respect that your neighbor has a heritage. We need to teach our youth that it is okay to want to learn of another culture and country and all that it stands for. African American history is not about slavery in America. We did not begin there. Our rich history is of great architects, inventors, craftsmen, kings, queens, and all other laymen who follow under our legacy of great builders. That is how our ancestors were found: building great pyramids, tombs, castles, and kingdoms that scientists all over the world marvel about to this very day. Let us all reach back to our beginnings and start a new way of living for our next generation and their children with the hope and goal that our world of war can become a world of peace. For as we know, the war that now presently exists in the Middle East after the tragedy of September 11 is in effect because another race and culture was not given the respect and support it felt it deserved. This war has caused a world financial crisis, suicide bombings, terrorist threats within our cities, and strain for government relations to come to a level of peace. Is this how we are going to end this beautiful world that was entrusted to us by God? The answer lies within you.

Written by Kevin Cavon

ATLANTA'S BLACK GAY PRIDE WEEKEND
"NOTHING TO BE PROUD ABOUT"

The city of Atlanta is undoubtedly one of our country's most beautiful cities; it is rich with culture and diversity. The thing I love the most about ATL is the open heart for its prominent and thriving gay community. San Francisco is a place where homosexuals went to live in peace; however, its culture is still, to this day, vast for the Caucasian gay community. Atlanta has given its gay and lesbian community the proverbial key to the city. Because of it, we prosper here greatly along with the large population of African Americans. We have prominent businesses; we complete degrees here, adopt, procreate, and raise children here and continue to grow in population. However, with all that greatness, the thing that alarms me is why we are growing in population. It could be for the wrong reasons.

So now I will show the draw of such events and, if not careful, what it can do to so many young men and women who are just beginning to figure out the direction for success in their lives.

Now of course, there are many other influences that would draw an individual to this city, that is, of an alternative lifestyle. Yet the one that has for so many years become the story of many is their visit during Atlanta Black Gay Pride Weekend. Now I will commend the literary and arts community—they always present and offer top-notch theater, book readings, and signings, as well as upscale events that display our culture in the arts. Yet not even that gains the attention of the masses like two other things that have become the meeting places for three nights of, for a lack of a better word, "self-induced suicide." They are the nightclubs and Piedmont Park. Thousands of brothers and sisters come from all over the nation if you can actually believe that. But it is true. However, our presentation of what this community truly stands for when they are not visiting is not presented. But what is presented is a great party life where at some clubs you can purchase drugs and use drugs; the stalls are consumed with in-and-out trysts. Young men and women from these different places set up dates with strangers and carry out "anything goes" style fantasies. Now of the mentality of this scene is now "Atlanta clubs are *hot*!" If you are a club head, drug addict, or explorer, this will appeal to you. Now the danger comes in what happens the rest of the night—unprotected sex, more drugs, sex parties, bath houses filled with those who are living the good life and those aspiring to do so, hustlers, and promiscuous brothers. I am not calling it out in malice. I was once a victim of the drug and club scene. I am just letting Atlanta's gay and lesbian community and those who wish to join it. Know that it is time to "clean up our act." It begins at home. Before these young people arrive, they are bombarded on the Internet with the stripper club events and the pool parties, and then they go on the Atlanta "sex sites" or chat rooms; they see who is hosting sex parties, which are, in my opinion, the source of so many diseases being transmitted at one time. I have never been to one. I would admit it if I had, but I do have friends and associates who have been in their past. And I will never recant my statement. In one night at one of these places, you can get HIV, syphilis, gonorrhea, and hepatitis. These happen to be the main things rampant in our community here in Atlanta. I am just keeping it real with everyone because some self-control and mature behaviors have to happen regarding sex or our younger generations are

going to spend much time in hospitals and early visits to the grave. It has already begun.

For this, I fault those who think that it's okay. It's not okay. Atlanta's African American male gay community outside of this city has gained a disturbing reputation for being a city of "hoes," PnP (party and play city)! I am just keeping it real.

I take pride in being a gentleman and having class. It offends me when I hear that, because most of my friends are the complete opposite. You all are a small percentage of our community who are wild like that. But it is your reputation that gets publicized and what HBO shows are made about. When I tell people as I travel they have the wrong perception of Atlanta gay males, they tell me why they don't. It always involves Pride Weekend. Let me tell you as I tell them. All of my friends—male, female, gay, or straight—in Atlanta hold degrees, hold public office, own homes (most of them), and many own their own businesses and are successful even during this recession. Don't be deceived—during pride weekend, a vast majority of us natives stay away from downtown, Lenox mall, and Piedmont Park. That's where I fall in. I stay away. Now to you out-of-towners, don't be deceived. The majority of us are not living here like it is sleepaway camp, living with this one and that one, working dead-end jobs. No, that is not the case, but that is what seems to happen to most of you when you, at the drop of dime with no planning, pack up and move here, then become a transient. My last ex-partner is now a transient, but he was when I met him. He did the same thing; came here, saw all these men, then thought, *Smorgasbord!* But he now has gotten a taste of what that wild lifestyle can do. He lost his job, home, and car, and he still continues to put his sexual needs before his livelihood.

You come here to live a peaceful, open lifestyle, but you forget before you are gay or lesbian, you are men and women first. And you have to be about your business or cease to exist here.

Come here with a plan and a job. Telling your family "I have a friend that is going to let me stay with them until I get a job" is not a plan. It's a recipe for eminent danger. I have helped a few of you during your transition periods, so I know. HIV/AIDS, syphilis, gonorrhea, and Hepatitis B is what having unprotected and drug-induced sex has to offer most of you, or if you want ways to commit suicide free of charge.

We who live here need to set better examples for who we say we are. And, my older gay brothers, we really have to step up and not only be examples but understand these young people don't need us as sex partners; they need us as mentors. They are failing life, and the most they can get out of us is sex and a few trinkets or a place to stay for a minute. We can make a difference in the direction of our community. Since when has it become okay to ruin someone else's life for your personal pleasure? It is time for our number of statistics to come down. I have had two partners who were HIV negative when we met and are HIV negative right now, to this day. We had full intimacy; we just did it maturely. I once said I would not want anyone who was not positive like me because a doctor told me it would be better. Love whom you choose and choose whom you love; just protect each other.

I close with only a few requests. Those who come here for Pride Weekend, respect our city and our hotels (keep your doors closed and your noise down, and our motels, don't trash them), expand your horizon, and visit things here that have nothing to do with being gay but being human. And if and when you do decide that this city is for you, you will know it was more than the great guy or girl you met, more than the hot nightlife that was only hot because so many out-of-towners made it that way.

And for the natives, let's work hard to protect those whose families we do not know and cannot see but know they love them more than we do. Send them home the same way they came—healthy and well. Peace.

Written by Kevin Cavon

IN A GUST OF WIND

(Blink of an Eye)

In a gust of wind and the blink of an eye, the picture changes.
Who is this person in the mirror, a stranger to everyone, a stranger to me?
He is darker, shorter, thinner, and weak. Can barely stand on his own. Dear Lord, is this me?
His thinking is slow, his speech impaired, his vision, hearing,
ability to use the right side of his body nearly gone.

In a gust of wind and the blink of an eye, the picture changes. *Crackle, pop, snap*—are
those my bones beneath my flesh? My God, are you here? Do you hear? Will you be here?
Picked up the phone to hang it again, can't tell no one. Afraid, alone, confused . . .
Alone?

In a gust of wind and the blink of an eye, the picture changes.
Snap! *Crackle*! *Pop*! Snap my bones back where they belong. *Crackle* is the
sound of the dried mucus, cold and fungus clinging to the bones.
Pop! The sound from within my back, my neck, and skull. Lord, it's been
over a year. I still hear this song. Lord, how long, how long?

I sound like me. I look like me. I do not feel like me. I recognize you. I know
it's you and you do not see me. How could that be? How could that be?
In a gust of wind and the blink of an eye, the picture changes.

Written by Kevin Cavon

To those of you who live daily with HIV and AIDS, don't stop living,
don't stop laughing, and don't stop loving . . . yourself!

WHERE DO YOU STAND?

Do you stand on a foundation made of strength andIntegrity?

Or do you stand on a foundation made up of weakness andDisloyalty?

When you look in the mirror, who and what do you see?
Are you fine being you, or would you rather be me?
Do you take life for the lesson it tries toTeach?

Or do you stand on big things and the small?
Where do you stand? Yes, I really want to know.From where
I'm standing, we all have a long way to go!

Written by Natarsia Joye-Lawrence

TODAY

(An Affirmation)

As we start the day
There are so many things going on
Why is it that we never just stop and listen to the quiet within?
Everyone and everything around becomesmore important than the inner peace that exists.

If we take the time to be still and listen to the flow of life through our veins
Or the strong force of adrenaline in our heart
Maybe things will not feel so burdensome
And all of our fears be would eliminated
So today, I've decide to sit and listen to the inner calm of life that begins within me

Early Christianity

Gentile, in the context of Early Christianity, meant "non-Jewish." It was a matter of dispute whether proselytization should be extended to the Gentiles (that is, the Greco-Roman population of the Roman Empire) or whether it should remain restricted to the Jewish communities throughout the Empire.

Attached to this question was the Circumcision controversy in early Christianity, i.e., does a gentile need to convert to Judaism before he can convert to Christianity? The position of the Judaizers was that this was a necessity, taking Christianity to remain fully within Judaism, including obedience to the Torah Laws. The opposite position was defended by Paul of Tarsus, who argued against the Judaizers. The Council of Jerusalem decided in favor of the more liberal position, allowing converts to forgo circumcision. This decision contributed to the rapid spread of Christianity; since it made Christianity a more attractive option for interested pagans than Rabbinic Judaism, which instituted a more stringent circumcision procedure in response. See Brit milah.

In the Bible

In Saint Jerome's Latin version of the Bible, the Vulgate, *gentilis* was used in this wider sense, along with *gentes*, to translate Greek and Hebrew words with similar meanings that referred to the non-Israelite peoples.

The most important of such Hebrew words was *goyim* (singular, *goy*), a term with the broad meaning of "peoples" or "nations," which was sometimes used to refer to Israelites, but most commonly as a generic label for other peoples. *Strong's Concordance* defines *goy* as "nation, people usually of non-Hebrew people, or of descendants of Abraham of Israel, or of a swarm of locusts or other animals; (fig.) Goyim = "nations" (*Strongs* #1471).[1]

In the KJV, *Gentile* is only one of several words used to translate "goy" or "goyim." It is translated as "nation" 374 times, "heathen" 143 times, "Gentiles" 30 times, and "people" 11 times. Some of these verses, such as Genesis 12:2 and Genesis 25:23, refer to Israelites or descendants of Abraham. Other verses, such as Isaiah 2:4 and Deuteronomy 11:23, are generic references to any nation. Typically, the KJV restricts the use of Gentile as a translation when the text is specifically referring to non-Israelites. For example, the only use of the word in Genesis is in chapter 10, verse 5, referring to the peopling of the world by descendants of Japheth, "By these were the isles of the Gentiles divided in their lands; every one after his tongue, after their families, in their nations."[2]

In the New Testament, the word translates Greek terms for peoples in general and is used specifically to indicate non-Jewish peoples, as in Jesus's command to the apostles in Matthew chapter 10.

> These twelve Jesus sent forth, and commanded them, saying, Go not into the way of the Gentiles, and into any city of the Samaritans enter ye not: But go rather to the lost sheep of the house of Israel.

Here, *Gentiles* becomes a synonym for pagan cultures of the period.

Altogether, the word is used 123 times in the King James Version of the Bible and 168 times in the New Revised Standard Version.

Modern Usage

As in the King James Bible, from the seventeenth century onward, *gentile* was most commonly used to refer to non-Jews. This was in the context of European Christian societies with a Jewish minority. For this reason, *Gentile* commonly meant persons brought up in the Christian faith, as opposed to the adherents of Judaism, and was not typically used to refer to non-Jews in non-Western cultures.

Pagans are generally defined as those who worship false gods. During Bible history, pagans were viewed with utter contempt, not because of who they were (since anyone who truly repented and turned to and obeyed God was accepted) but because of what they did: "living in debauchery, lust, drunkenness, orgies, carousing and detestable idolatry" (1 Peter 4:3, NIV).

What Did Jesus Christ Say About Pagans?

"So do not worry, saying, 'What shall we eat?' or 'What shall we drink?' or 'What shall we wear?' For the pagans run after all these things, and your heavenly Father knows that you need them. But seek first His kingdom and His righteousness, and all these things will be given to you as well" (Matthew 6:31–33, NIV).

"But when you pray, go into your room, close the door and pray to your Father, Who is unseen. Then your Father, Who sees what is done in secret, will reward you. And when you pray, do not keep on babbling like pagans, for they think they will be heard because of their many words. Do not be like them, for your Father knows what you need before you ask Him" (Matthew 6:6–8, NIV).

"If your brother sins against you go and show him his fault, just between the two of you. If he listens to you, you have won your brother over. But if he will not listen, take one or two others along, so that 'every matter may be established by the testimony of two or three witnesses.' If he refuses to listen to them, tell it to the church; and if he refuses to listen even to the church, treat him as you would a pagan or a tax collector" (Matthew 18:15–17, NIV).

"He causes His sun to rise on the evil and the good, and sends rain on the righteous and the unrighteous. If you love those who love you, what reward will you get? Are not even the tax collectors doing that? And if you greet only your brothers, what are you doing more than others? Do not even pagans do that?" (Matthew 5:45–47, NIV).

Greetings in the name of God our Father. I am not an ordained minister nor evangelist. I am not a scientist, just merely a man who has been in the church and has known who God is in my life since I was five years of age. I have never been confused of whether God loved me or not, in spite of this cruel world. I often wondered if God ever had anything positive to say about people who were born in a manner in which He knew before we were born what we were going to be. It is not a choice. Who would choose to ridiculed, black sheep, beaten, and kicked out of organizations, refused job positions, and murdered by gay and lesbian haters? I now say to you, thank you for your transgressions, trials, and tribulations you have inflicted on us. I now understand why we are such a blessed culture of people. It is now through Romans we can see that God did seek redemption for our souls through Jesus's death. We were not left out as many pastors, preachers, and sign-holding haters may believe. You all have singled out our sin, calling it homosexuality, when in fact, that is not the sin, no more than the term *heterosexuality*. The sin is still and always will be fornication, sex outside of marriage!

God has now given me authority to do a thing that very few, if any, preachers have ever done. I am not going to preach from a scripture nor a verse. I will be coming from the entire book of Romans. I challenge anyone who wants to come against me—keep in mind, not you, your ministry, nor one thousand of you preachers, if you come together in protest—you cannot now deny God's Word. I did not make it up! Even you said everything in the Bible is true. So fall back, and you yourself may learn some things.

I was listening to one of my favorite gospel radio shows hosted by the Co Co Brother, when a gentleman came on with a very disgusted, angry tone in his voice. "For all you gay folks, read Romans 1!" and then he hung up. I had heard enough of God's disdain for it in Deuteronomy and Leviticus. I was totally taken aback. I said, "God, not even murderers get treated as badly as we do in the church or anywhere else. I guess you truly do hate us, whom you said you created, and no one else but you knew us before we knew ourselves." But God said, "No, read it all. Not only do I want you to read it, but I also want you to interpret it for your life and the others." I was not only stunned by what I read after reading the entire book, but I said to myself, obviously, like so many others, we stop at whatever we are told or guided to read. This causes so many of us to not only be ignorant but also go against God's will, knowingly passing judgment and condemning people into hell without the *power* of God to do so. This message is for everyone who has been afflicted by so-called saints of God and also the saints of God who have doubted God's love for us: the drug addict, the whore, and her children; fornicators, straight or gay! We are the Gentiles of this day! But thank God for the revelation through Jesus's Apostle Paul! We do have a way of living that would be pleasing to God, but we still must turn our life over to Him. After this, I pray mercy on the souls of anyone who harms another person who is not like them with their tongue or stands in judgment. I do not expect everyone to receive this revelation from God, but I will say this: the interpreter Paul of this book of Romans was once a deceiver. Jesus made him an apostle, and God made him a saint. So who can say whom God reveals His omnipotence to? No one. I interpret as Har'rell because it is my name that is from the Hebrew word *Harel*, meaning "Mountain of God"! I now give to you:

MY VERY FIRST AND VERY LAST SERMON
THE BOOK OF ROMANS SAVES US ALL!

Romans 1 (Contemporary English Version)
Romans 1
From Paul, a servant of Christ Jesus

God chose me to be an apostle, and he appointed me to preach the good news that he promised long ago by what his prophets said in the Holy Scriptures. This good news is about his Son, our Lord Jesus Christ! As a human, he was from the family of David. But the Holy Spirit proved that Jesus is the powerful Son of God, because he was raised from death. Jesus was kind to me and chose me to be an apostle, so that people of all nations would obey and have faith. You

are some of those people chosen by Jesus Christ. This letter is to all of you in Rome. God loves you and has chosen you to be his very own people.

I pray that God our Father and our Lord Jesus Christ will be kind to you and will bless you with peace!

A Prayer of Thanks

First, I thank God in the name of Jesus Christ for all of you. I do this because people everywhere in the world are talking about your faith. God has seen how I never stop praying for you, while I serve him with all my heart and tell the good news about his Son.

In all my prayers, I ask God to make it possible for me to visit you. I want to see you and share with you the same blessings that God's Spirit has given me. Then you will grow stronger in your faith. What I am saying is that we can encourage each other by the faith that is ours.

My friends, I want you to know that I have often planned to come for a visit. But something has always kept me from doing it. I want to win followers to Christ in Rome, as I have done in many other places. It doesn't matter if people are civilized and educated or if they are uncivilized and uneducated. I must tell the good news to everyone. That's why I am eager to visit all of you in Rome.

The Power of the Good News

I am proud of the good news! It is God's powerful way of saving all people who have faith, whether they are Jews or Gentiles. The good news tells how God accepts everyone who has faith, but only those who have faith. It is just as the Scriptures say, "The people God accepts because of their faith will live."

Har'rell: Paul obviously had been given a tremendous word for his people. However, if we look at our lives today, he is still speaking these things to us. At one point, we who are heterosexual feel that as long as you are lying with the opposite sex, then you have grace from God even if you are not married. Huh? We hold fast to what we want out of Old Testament teachings to secure our stagnant beliefs and ignore the changes God made in the Word only based on the death of Jesus. Romans, a book only a few books away

from revelations, reveals to us a God who wants us all, in spite of ourselves. God defines the word *testament* as "a covenant between us and Him." Now God is saying, when will we begin viewing the Old Testament as our old covenant with Him, really look at the sign of the times, and begin to truly teach of His new covenant to guide all of His children to Him, not by casting out in the church and media but by love, understanding, and His laws, which we break daily? To gain wisdom of peace within the New Testament, in which He gave us orders to keep order and control of ourselves in this, our new world, we created of technology and contemporary thoughts as our new covenant with Him. We have gone so far with our technology that we now think we have pinpointed the day of the world's end. I watch the *History* and *Discovery* channel, and I saw the movie *2012*. As vivid and true as that may have seemed, we just don't know how and when; that is still based on our level of thinking. God's thoughts surpasses what our mind can achieve regarding that day. But have faith in Him that when that day comes, you will be caught up to meet Him. However, understand now is the time for us to see what it is in ourselves we may be secretly guilty of, and repent of those things; consecrate and turn them over to Him.

Everyone Is Guilty

From heaven, God shows how angry he is with all the wicked and evil things that sinful people do to crush the truth. They know everything that can be known about God, because God has shown it all to them. God's eternal power and character cannot be seen. But from the beginning of creation, God has shown what these are like by all he has made. That's why those people don't have any excuse. They know about God, but they don't honor him or even thank him. Their thoughts are useless, and their stupid minds are in the dark. They claim to be wise, but they are fools. They don't worship the glorious and eternal God. Instead, they worship idols that are made to look like humans who cannot live forever, and like birds, animals, and reptiles.

Har'rell: Let me go here first . . . "Let him without sin cast the first stone!" Pastors, I hate to say this: God is speaking to you. You are given tremendous knowledge of what's in these scriptures, and yet souls are still confused, shouting on a moment and forgetting from week to week what they are being taught. God has equipped you preachers with so much knowledge, especially the pastor, and now is the time to release a wave of God like never before. Begin to educate now from the books the entire chapters of the book as it is written; there are revelations and rhema in a series flow to teach truly where God has us as a people and where we need to go. Now as far as the sinful things that we do are concerned, which we may not pay attention to, please understand God hates any sin just as much as He abhors same-gender sex. Well, let's see, let go to the Ten Commandments. Now I am just going to point them out all over again, and if it's you anywhere in there, go back and read verses 18 through 23. He is talking to you.

The Ten Commandments
(Exodus 20:2–17, NKJV)

1 I am the Lord your God, who brought you out of the land of Egypt, out of the house of bondage. You shall have no other gods before Me.

2 You shall not make for yourself a carved image, or any likeness of anything that is in heaven above, or that is in the earth beneath, or that is in the water under the earth; you shall not bow down to them nor serve them. For I, the Lord your God, am a jealous God, visiting the iniquity of the fathers on the children to the third and fourth generations of those who hate Me, but showing mercy to thousands, to those who love Me and keep My Commandments.

3 You shall not take the name of the Lord your God in vain, for the Lord will not hold him guiltless who takes His name in vain.

4 Remember the Sabbath day, to keep it holy. Six days you shall labor and do all your work, but the seventh day is the Sabbath of the Lord your God. In it you shall do no work: you, nor your son, nor your daughter, nor your male servant, nor your female servant, nor your cattle, nor your stranger who is within your gates. For in six days the Lord made the heavens and the earth, the sea, and all that is in them, and rested the seventh day. Therefore the Lord blessed the Sabbath day and hallowed it.

5 Honor your father and your mother, that your days may be long upon the land which the Lord Your God is giving you.

6 You shall not murder.

7   You shall not commit adultery.

8   You shall not steal.

9   You shall not bear false witness against your neighbor.

10   You shall not covet your neighbor's house; you shall not covet your neighbor's wife, nor his male servant, nor his female servant, nor his ox, nor his donkey, nor anything that is your neighbor's.

So God let these people go their own way. They did what they wanted to do, and their filthy thoughts made them do shameful things with their bodies. They gave up the truth about God for a lie, and they worshiped God's creation instead of God, who will be praised forever. Amen.

Har'rell: Now I understand this as it relates to Sodom and Gomorrah; however, here, the people knew He existed, but chose to glorify themselves by yielding to their desires. There were more persons during that time who were heterosexual and did the same things mentioned at the end of chapter one. So this verse did not discriminate. Instead of seeking truth here, now we are revealed the truth to our salvation in God. If God has given you over to a depraved mind, the devil has full license to bring into your life the lusts of your heart because those are his only gifts; he can't give you eternal life or happiness on earth. His (Satan's) happiness given to you always has a price. Usually it's your demise. When the temptation to commit a sin comes your way, remember you should recognize that because it did not come from God, it can only end in destruction because that is all Satan is capable of doing. Give us instant or temporary gratification. Look how many celebrities sold their souls to the devil and then right when they thought they had it all, Satan exposes their indiscretions to the world then takes it all back! When temptation comes, think about the price you have to pay when it's over. Before you think about how good it's going to make you feel, walk away and watch God begin to remove the desire. But you have to first show God that you can walk away. Read on . . .

God let them follow their own evil desires. Women no longer wanted to have sex in a natural way, and they did things with each other that were not natural. Men behaved in the same way. They stopped wanting to have sex with women and had strong desires for sex with other men. They did shameful things with each other, and what has happened to them is punishment for their foolish deeds.

Har'rell: Hold on. That sounds like today? I could be wrong, but I am not. Homosexuals almost never desire the opposite sex even, from childhood, so this was not referring to those born that way. Allow me to make it clearer—we were turned over to sin by the disobedience of Eve, and since that day when Eve made the decision to disobey God, neither she nor other women were given the ability of a perfect conception. So now we have children born disabled, autistic, with homosexual genetics, mental challenges (retardation), blind, and so much else. In other words, it takes a heterosexual person to create and or procreate a homosexual human. We are your seed, straight men, that grows in your womb, straight women, and yet you turn against us right in the presence of the eyes of God. God is saying it is no different than casting out any of the other imperfect births. Well, read on. I know you don't believe it and have already interpreted it another way. I know God said you would right at this very point; that's why we are going through the entire book of Romans. This is only the beginning.

So now let me speak to you, husbands and wives. I could see how you easily placed this on the homosexual community, but God is not speaking to us here. He is talking to you heterosexuals who have destroyed the union of marriage, women emasculating your husband in front of your friends and children, thinking you are better than him because you make more than him. You use sex as a control mechanism or take it away as a form of punishment. Men, you beat her, cheat on her, have other children with other women then have her help in raising them; you disown the children you bore with her with no communication. So unfortunately, you all find your solace in our community of people, the ones whom you thought of as pagans, gentiles, or Samaritans. Because although you stand with the crowd when the lights are on, you cry on our shoulders when no one else is watching. You borrow from us our money, clothing, and living places and behind closed doors have relations with us. Yet we do not blame you; we just show you love. Yet had it not been for you, we would not

be this way, nor would an entire world despise and condemn us. So begin with owning that fact.

Since these people refused even to think about God, he let their useless minds rule over them. That's why they do all sorts of indecent things. They are evil, wicked, and greedy, as well as mean in every possible way. They want what others have, and they murder, argue, cheat, and are hard to get along with. They gossip, say cruel things about others, and hate God. They are proud, conceited, and boastful, always thinking up new ways to do evil.

These people don't respect their parents. They are stupid, unreliable, and don't have any love or pity for others. They know God has said that anyone who acts this way deserves to die. But they keep on doing evil things, and they even encourage others to do them.

Har'rell: Now that we are clear whom God is speaking to, let us now focus on the redemption of us all because now we understand that He is not talking to those who had no choice in how they were born and live to seek him; He is speaking to those who walked away from marriage in exchange for drugs and illicit sex, as well as so many other immoral things. You have fashioned our lifestyle on television and on the radio airways for your benefit but then ridicule and show hate toward us, call us freaks, and think that we are perverse. We are not the ones who are perverse. You all began porn and have numerous sex brothels, swing and strip clubs, peep shows, all up and down the highways and in the community where we raise our children, and you call homosexuals perverse. A child at age seven can read a sign that says "XXX LIVE NUDE GIRLS" or "Adult Gentleman's Club" as he or she may be walking home from school. It is you, our straight society, that gives our children reason to explore dark places. Then you want to say something as ludicrous as "Gay marriage is going to harm our children." Get real, how many Christian creepers are roaming in these places at night? Are you one? Then judge you not, lest you be judged.

The gay and lesbian community has taken the blame for so many things that were not true. Yet we are still a loving, caring, and giving community. We are not proud, we do not boast, and we do not disrespect our parents, especially when they love on us in spite of our sexuality. And God knows we are not known to be or exposed to be murderers. I heard Donnie McClurkin recently preach a sermon that stated, "They are converting our children to their lifestyle, drawing them into their world of deception and lies." He had the sound of sorrow in his voice, but the message held no real merit. Neither I nor any friends of mine have ever gone out and tried to convert straight folks. I respect Pastor Donnie, and I thank God for his testimony of deliverance from sex with men; however you cannot be delivered from heterosexuality, so if he believes he is no longer homosexual, that's fine. Abstinence does not change your natural birth imperfection. A retarded person can learn to speak and function normally; however, he or she is still mentally retarded because they were born that way. I am not trying to challenge the pastor; I am just making sure we don't develop a new society of ignorant believers and haters.

Romans 2 (Contemporary English Version)
God's Judgment Is Fair

Some of you accuse others of doing wrong. But there is no excuse for what you do. When you judge others, you condemn yourselves, because you are guilty of doing the very same things. We know that God is right to judge everyone who behaves in this way. Do you really think God won't punish you, when you behave exactly like the people you accuse? You surely don't think much of God's wonderful goodness or of his patience and willingness to put up with you. Don't you know that the reason God is good to you is because he wants you to turn to him?

Har'rell: Let's break here. I was watching CNN summer 2009, and on the screen were several African-American pastors and preachers, in Washington, DC, at a bill hearing for gay marriage. They seemed irate and volatile in their stance. To say they were representing God and His views would have been a blasphemy to God. He did not send them to pass judgment, which is what they did. They showed tremendous hate in their heart. How can you preach "Love your neighbor as you love yourself" and show hate for a whole community? Are homosexuals excluded from being your neighbors?

Now let me speak directly to you African-American saved and unsaved folk. We have been and continue to be an oppressed people. Of all of the races I have spent time with, our race is the only race that hurts each other based on the light or dark complexion of our skin, economic status (yeah, we like to turn up our noses at those less fortunate when we think we have arrived), and we are the worst when it comes to accepting our homosexual brother, sister, son, or daughter. We are cruel and ungodly toward one another, and we are getting worse. We talk about the Mexicans are taking our jobs—no, they aren't! Your lazy butt was sleeping when you should have been at work. You called in sick two out of the five days you were supposed to work. You find excuses to leave before your shift ends, and you want to blame the Mexican who shows up early, leaves late, and does not complain until he or she gets home, never calls in unless he or she is really ill, and follows directions during work. How many of us do you see who have carpenter or plumber skills standing at a Home Depot looking for work daily? Not many. So stop complaining and rise up as a race. Right now, as far as I am concerned, the kind of race African Americans have become is a disgrace race because we disrespected the grace that God has showered over us. After all we endured as a people, we disgrace God by hurting each other. God is trying to bless us as a people, and instead of seeing His works through our new president, we continue to falter in our communities. Build up your neighbor, and God will build you up as well.

But you are stubborn and refuse to turn to God. So you are making things even worse for yourselves on that day when he will show how angry he is and will judge the world with fairness. God will reward each of us for what we have done. He will give eternal life to everyone who has patiently done what is good in the hope of receiving glory, honor, and life that lasts forever. But he will show how angry and furious he can be with every selfish person who rejects the truth and wants to do evil. All who are wicked will be punished with trouble and suffering. It doesn't matter if they are Jews or Gentiles. But all who do right will be rewarded with glory, honor, and peace, whether they are Jews or Gentiles. God doesn't have any favorites!

Har'rell: Here again, God is to telling everyone, not just homosexuals, you have no right to judge anyone, especially during a time such as this. Would it not be more important to focus on what you can do to aid this economy, aid a person with your resources who is in need, begin going to your children's schools and finding out why they are getting such lackluster education, or volunteer in your community? Anything that is going to make a positive impact on someone else's life. We have become a country so divided, so full of hate and disdain for each other that we cannot produce nor progress past where we are now. And I am referring to those in Christ especially. We assume we are ready for His return—newsflash, God has said, from the pastor to the pews, there has to be deliverance, repentance, and forgiveness. Our largest of churches have the least true faith and understanding of totally what it is to love as God loves you. You don't even say "Have a good afternoon" to the person you sat next to after service is over! And you believe you are showing God love? You have missed the mark. Yet God is still coming. Are you sure you're ready?

Those people who don't know about God's Law will still be punished for what they do wrong. And the Law will be used to judge everyone who knows what it says. God accepts those who obey his Law, but not those who simply hear it.

Some people naturally obey the Law's commands, even though they don't have the Law. This proves that the conscience is like a law written in the human heart. And it will show whether we are forgiven or condemned, when God appoints

Jesus Christ to judge everyone's secret thoughts, just as my message says.

Har'rell: I just want you to read verses 12 through 16 twice, then read them once more. Selah.

The Jews and the Law

Some of you call yourselves Jews. You trust in the Law and take pride in God. By reading the Scriptures, you learn how God wants you to behave, and you discover what is right. You are sure that you are a guide for the blind and a light for all who are in the dark. And since there is knowledge and truth in God's Law, you think you can instruct fools and teach young people.

But how can you teach others when you refuse to learn? You preach that it is wrong to steal. But do you steal? You say people should be faithful in marriage. But are you faithful? You hate idols, yet you rob their temples. You take pride in the Law, but you disobey the Law and bring shame to God. It is just as the Scriptures tell us, "You have made foreigners say insulting things about God."

Har'rell: In other words, Christians, we are not living holy and acceptable lives. We shield our mess with appearances, walk in church with our diva-tude on, but when the camera is off, we are anything but an example of God. We are not loving toward one another. We do not practice not only what we preach but also what is preached to us. And those who are unsaved do not see a reason to come to Christ because we show them how worldly we really are. In the workplace, we quote scriptures to them, but when things don't go our way, we curse and yell at the top of our lungs. Some of us even threaten to get physical. We are bringing shame to God as Christians, and moreover, forget denomination—all of us who believe in God in any language are disappointing the Father, individually and collectively. Now those who don't know God talk about us in a way that suggests, "If this is how you act and you are saved, why should I come to your church? I act better than you unsaved." Remember what God said in verse 14: some of them obey His laws and don't even know it.

Being circumcised (**saved**) is worthwhile, if you obey the Law. But if you don't obey the Law, you are no better off than people who are not circumcised (**saved**). In fact, if they obey the Law, they are as good as anyone who is circumcised (**saved**). So everyone who obeys the Law, but has never been circumcised (**saved**), will condemn you. Even though you are circumcised (**saved**) and have the Law, you still don't obey its teachings.

Just because you live like a Jew and are circumcised (**saved**) doesn't make you a real Jew. To be a real Jew you must obey the Law. True circumcision (**salvation**) is something that happens deep in your heart, not something done to your body. And besides, you should want praise from God and not from humans.

Har'rell: I exchanged the words in order to give us a clear understanding of what God is saying in this time. Not in the '70s, '80s, or '90s when you preached from this scripture. There are folk who don't go to church and worship God daily. They have not taken the right hand of fellowship anywhere. they have not go down the aisle for altar call, and they have not found a home church and are not looking for one, and God has not led them to do so. The love and obedience that He receives from them, he keeps them away from being corrupted by doctrines, new religious orders, and dissention in the church. My mother has done her own home service every Sunday for over thirty years! I don't knock her. She is a prayer warrior and a servant of God. She heals hearts, mends spirits, and calms souls with every power that God has given her. I definitely don't want her in today's church! What is the law? Love one another as you love yourself and as God loves you!

Ask yourself, "How often do I break this law? Daily?"

Romans 3

What good is it to be a Jew? What good is it to be circumcised? It is good in a lot of ways! First of all, God's messages were spoken to the Jews. It is true that some of them did not believe the message. But does this mean that God cannot be trusted, just because they did not have faith? No, indeed! God tells the truth, even if everyone else is a liar. The Scriptures say about God.

Har'rell: Just because you may not believe that this is, thus saith the Lord. God is saying, "So what! I don't care what you think. I know you are a bishop, I know you have been pasturing for twenty years—so what? For twenty years you have preached from scriptures when I have wanted my children to learn of me Book by Book as it was written, from beginning to end." There is

enough in one book of God's Word to carry a series of sermons for several months. And it will fall right in line with where God is calling your ministry to be. Souls will be more understanding of the realm of God and how it operates in the earthly realm.

"Your words will be proven true, and in court you will win your case."

If our evil deeds show how right God is, then what can we say? Is it wrong for God to become angry and punish us? What a foolish thing to ask. But the answer is, "No." Otherwise, how could God judge the world? Since your lies bring great honor to God by showing how truthful he is, you may ask why God still says you are a sinner. You might as well say, "Let's do something evil, so that something good will come of it!" Some people even claim that we are saying this. But God is fair and will judge them as well.

Har'rell: See, I told you—God is fair and just. However, some Christians want God to be this villain who hates homosexuals. God told me He never said that; He loves all His children. Sex with two men or two women disgraces God; the act is an abomination. However, read on because since the Old Testament, God has issued a level of grace to those born different, called Jews or Gentiles, and those mistreated, though they can still be who they are in Christ. This grace is because they love God, serve God, and are used as vessels to increase God's kingdom as everyone else who is saved.

109

No One Is Good

What does all this mean? Does it mean that we Jews are better off than the Gentiles? No, it doesn't! Jews, as well as Gentiles, are ruled by sin, just as I have said. The Scriptures tell us, "No one is acceptable to God!

Not one of them understands or even searches for God. They have all turned away and are worthless. There isn't one person who does right. Their words are like an open pit, and their tongues are good only for telling lies. Each word is as deadly as the fangs of a snake, and they say nothing but bitter curses. These people quickly become violent. Wherever they go, they leave ruin and destruction.

They don't know how to live in peace. They don't even fear God.

Har'rell: If this sounds like someone you know, I have news for you: it just might be you.

We know that everything in the Law was written for those who are under its power. The Law says these things to stop anyone from making excuses and to let God show that the whole world is guilty. God doesn't accept people simply because they obey the Law. No, indeed! All the Law does is to point out our sin.

Har'rell: Do you hate your brother? Do you not speak to your neighbor? If your neighbor needs help, do you help him or look the other way? Do you show love in all you do? Do you love your boss at work? Or do you wish hate on him for reprimanding you! Do you accept people for who they are and how they were created?

God's Way of Accepting People

Now we see how God does make us acceptable to him. The Law and the Prophets tell how we become acceptable, and it isn't by obeying the Law of Moses. God treats everyone alike. He accepts people only because they have faith in Jesus Christ. All of us have sinned and fallen short of God's glory. But God treats us much better than we deserve, and because of Christ Jesus, he freely accepts us and sets us free from our sins. God sent Christ to be our sacrifice. Christ offered his life's blood, so that by faith in him we could come to God. And God did this to show that in the past he was right to be patient and forgive sinners. This also shows that God is right when he accepts people who have faith in Jesus. What is left for us to brag about? Not a thing! Is it because we obeyed some law? No! It is because of faith. We see that people are acceptable to God because they have faith, and not because they obey the Law. Does God belong only to the Jews? Isn't he also the God of the Gentiles? Yes, he is! There is only one God, and he accepts Gentiles as well as Jews, simply because of their faith. Do we destroy the Law by our faith? Not at all! We make it even more powerful.

Har'rell: Now let's go back to those who are in the church and are homosexual. We accepted Jesus as our Lord and Savior. We pay our tithes; we have the faith that God has called us to have in Him to do all things exceedingly and abundantly all we can think or ask. So if we are saying that everyone is the same in the eyes of God, how dare you say differently from the pulpit! How can you teach others to isolate and hate the homosexual when God loves him or her no differently than he loves you and will judge him or her no differently than He judges you? Yet you have made an entire nation of people feel inferior and depraved of God. But thank God you are not God.

Romans 4 (Contemporary English Version)
The Example of Abraham

Well then, what can we say about our ancestor Abraham? If he became acceptable to God because of what he did, then he would have something to brag about. But he would never be able to brag about it to God. The Scriptures say, "God accepted Abraham because Abraham had faith in him."

Money paid to workers isn't a gift. It is something they earn by working. But you cannot make God accept you because of something you do. God accepts sinners only because they have faith in him. In the Scriptures David talks about the blessings that come to people who are acceptable to God, even though they don't do anything to deserve these blessings. David says, "God blesses people whose sins are forgiven and whose evil deeds are forgotten. The Lord blesses people whose sins are erased from his book."

Har'rell: Now I want to talk to you who are homosexual, it is time to clean up your acts because we do fall under the same laws. However, God is now giving us favor to live an acceptable life unto Him. Many of you feel that we can have sex with any and everyone and because of the inflictions you have the grace of god to do so. No, you do not. Many of us are promiscuous; we use drugs to engage in group sex and many other indecent behaviors. I know—I was once guilty, using the Internet to look for immediate gratification. But did you know that each time you engage in this behavior, you move further away from God and closer to the grasp of Satan and his wickedness? If you are homosexual and are having sex outside of marriage, God will judge you based on your sin of fornication. If you are committed and vowed to one partner, your union is a union between two individuals who have faith in God. That is now His gift to us; have faith in Him, and your sins are forgiven. I go deeper into this in later chapters. But just know I am not finished with this particular subject of marriage. It belongs to God, not to man, and the only part of it that belongs to the church is the ceremony of holy matrimony. I know you can't believe right now that God's ways are this far away from yours nor are His thoughts . . . only if it benefits your beliefs, as well as what you despise.

Are these blessings meant for circumcised people or for those who are not circumcised? Well, the Scriptures say that God accepted Abraham because Abraham had faith in him. But when did this happen? Was it before or after Abraham was circumcised? Of course, it was before.

Abraham let himself be circumcised to show that he had been accepted because of his faith even before he was circumcised. This makes Abraham the father of all who are acceptable to God because of their faith, even though they are not circumcised. This also makes Abraham the father of everyone who is circumcised and has faith in God, as Abraham did before he was circumcised.

This is another area in which if you exchange the word cir-

cumcised to the word *saved*, you would gain clarity.

The Promise Is for All Who Have Faith

God promised Abraham and his descendants that he would give them the world. This promise wasn't made because Abraham had obeyed a law, but because his faith in God made him acceptable. If Abraham and his descendants were given this promise because they had obeyed a law, then faith would mean nothing, and the promise would be worthless.

Har'rell: Without faith, it is impossible to please God. We say it, but do we really live it? But by having said faith, it makes us acceptable, yet we doubt God's ability to bring us out, to change our situation, or even have faith that what He is commanding us to do is truly from Him, for us to obey. By why would He not want us to love one another as the Law requires us to do? Would that not be being more like Jesus? WWJD faded from our memory very fast. One minute it was on our shirts, our cars, on our screensavers at work, and used as a cliché to get others to do right or make right choices. Now we are so caught up on WWID—"What would I do?" We couldn't care less about being Christ-like. God's Law is not being revealed in us, and He is becoming very angry with our leaders and those under them. You are more interested in what you are wearing on Sunday than the message God wants you to receive.

God becomes angry when his Law is broken. But where there isn't a law, it cannot be broken. Everything depends on having faith in God, so that God's promise is assured by his great kindness. This promise isn't only for Abraham's descendants who have the Law. It is for all who are Abraham's descendants because they have faith, just as he did. Abraham is the ancestor of us all. The Scriptures say that Abraham would become the ancestor of many nations. This promise was made to Abraham because he had faith in God, who raises the dead to life and creates new things.

God promised Abraham a lot of descendants. And when it all seemed hopeless, Abraham still had faith in God and became the ancestor of many nations. Abraham's faith never became weak, not even when he was nearly a hundred years old. He knew that he was almost dead and that his wife Sarah could not have children. But Abraham never doubted or questioned God's promise. His faith made him strong, and he gave all the credit to God.

Har'rell: God has promised you visions to come to pass, marriages, children, businesses, jobs, and so many other great things, but your faith has not paralleled with your works. Yes, He has promised you these things, but without faith and your works toward your faith, you cannot make these things come to pass. It is your faith walk that God will recognize, and through your obedience to walk in faith do you receive the promises of God.

Abraham was certain that God could do what he had promised. So God accepted him, just as we read in the Scriptures. But these words were not written only for Abraham. They were written for us, since we will also be accepted because of our faith in God, who raised our Lord Jesus to life. God gave Jesus to die for our sins, and

112

he raised him to life, so that we would be made acceptable to God.

Romans 5 (Contemporary English Version)
What It Means to Be Acceptable to God

By faith, we have been made acceptable to God. And now, because of our Lord Jesus Christ, we live at peace with God. Christ has also introduced us to God's undeserved kindness on which we take our stand. So we are happy, as we look forward to sharing in the glory of God. But that's not all! We gladly suffer, because we know that suffering helps us to endure. And endurance builds character, which gives us a hope that will never disappoint us. All of this happens because God has given us the Holy Spirit, who fills our hearts with his love. Christ died for us at a time when we were helpless and sinful. No one is really willing to die for an honest person, though someone might be willing to die for a truly good person. But God showed how much he loved us by having Christ die for us, even though we were sinful.

But there is more! Now that God has accepted us because Christ sacrificed his life's blood, we will also be kept safe from God's anger. Even when we were God's enemies, he made peace with us, because his Son died for us. Yet something even greater than friendship is ours. Now that we are at peace with God, we will be saved by his Son's life. And in addition to everything else, we are happy because God sent our Lord Jesus Christ to make peace with us.

Har'rell: We have to make sure that we understand God's change of heart, or should I say "change of wrath," in the New Testament to make it plainer. In the Old Testament before the birth of Christ, God saw us who did not believe in Him or have faith in Him as an enemy; our sins had no covering. After the death of Christ, it's like a father taking the time out to understand the child's perspective and saying, "Because I can see it your way, as long as you trust me to be your guide and have faith in me to make the right pathways for you to walk toward your destiny, then I will give you peace and favor to get the job done, as well as live a life that is acceptable unto God."

Adam and Christ

Adam sinned, and that sin brought death into the world. Now everyone has sinned, and so everyone must die. Sin was in the world before the Law came. But no record of sin was kept, because there was no Law. Yet death still had power over all who lived from the time of Adam to the time of Moses. This happened, though not everyone disobeyed a direct command from God, as Adam did.

In some ways Adam is like Christ who came later. But the gift that God was kind enough to give was very different from Adam's sin. That one sin brought death to many others. Yet in an even greater way, Jesus Christ alone brought God's gift of kindness to many people.

Har'rell: Now this scripture validates what I just said previously: how after Christ, God's kindness to His children became greater in so many ways into existence. Much of who we are, good or evil, has to do with the formulation of the characters in Adam and in Eve.

There is a lot of difference between Adam's sin and God's gift. That one sin led to punishment. But God's gift made it possible for us to be acceptable to him, even though we have sinned many times. Death ruled like a king because Adam had sinned. But that cannot compare with what Jesus Christ has done. God has been so kind to us, and he has accepted us because of Jesus. And so we will live and rule like kings.

Har'rell: We are all sinners who in God's eye sin daily, but because of Jesus, He accepts us in spite of our sin. How do we live and rule like kings? you ask. We take for granted the things that others do not have. We call our homes our castle; we rule over that domain and everyone in it. As long as we are good stewards over it, we get to reign as king and queen. That is just the home; now add the business or the high-paying position that affords you people working under you, whom God allows you to have rule over.

Everyone was going to be punished because Adam sinned. But because of the good thing that Christ has done, God accepts us and gives us the gift of life. Adam disobeyed God and caused many others to be sinners. But Jesus obeyed him and will make many people acceptable to God.

Har'rell: God does not have to tell me over and over again the same thing, but observe how many times He has said this, that because of Jesus, He accepts us and gives us all the gift of life.

The Law came, so that the full power of sin could be seen. Yet where sin was powerful, God's kindness was even more powerful. Sin ruled by means of death. But God's kindness now rules, and God has accepted us because of Jesus Christ our Lord. This means that we will have eternal life.

Romans 6 (Contemporary English Version)
Dead to Sin but Alive Because of Christ

What should we say? Should we keep on sinning, so that God's wonderful kindness will show up even better? No, we should not! If we are dead to sin, how can we go on sinning? Don't you know that all who share in Christ Jesus by being baptized also share in his death? When we were baptized, we died and were buried with Christ. We were baptized, so that we would live a new life, as Christ was raised to life by the glory of God the Father.

Har'rell: Many of us may feel, "Well, let me live according to how I feel cause God has my back, and He will take me back whenever I am ready." What God is saying is yes, you are right, He will take you back, but when you return, you will be broken, bruised, lost, empty, and wounded because while you are in His permissive will, the divine order of your life is not being fulfilled and you are without covering. So in order to live a peaceful and productive life while you are here on earth, live according to the law of Christ. Love one another as you love yourself.

If we shared in Jesus' death by being baptized, we will be raised to life with him. We know that the persons we used to be were nailed to the cross with Jesus. This was done, so that our sinful bodies would no longer be the slaves of sin. We know that sin doesn't have power over dead people.

As surely as we died with Christ, we believe we will also live with him. We know that death no longer has any power over Christ. He died and was raised to life, never again to die. When Christ died, he died for sin once and for all. But now he is alive, and he lives only for God. [11]In the same way, you must think of yourselves as dead to the power of sin. But Christ Jesus has given life to you, and you live for God.

Har'rell: I want to speak specifically here to the homosexual male community. Not to say that lesbians do not participate to some degree in what I am about to address, but it is more prevalent in the gay male community, primarily African American males but not solely. Just because you are homosexual does not make you a sinner—it makes you born of sin—so any degree of birth defects or imperfect births becomes possible. Now where you are a sinner is in the way you live promiscuously, drug-induced sexual immorality. Fornication with a male and female, male and male, or female and female does not change the definition—it is still a sin. I beseech you, especially you twenty- to thirty-year-olds, to seek a more productive and respectable life. If you attend bathhouses like the Den or Flex or any others in other cities, you are setting yourself up for suicide. It is not healthy nor safe to place yourself in situations with strangers wherein you do not know their history or sexual past. All you know is "I am high and this feels good," but then you get a report that you have syphilis or HIV or some other sexually transmitted disease. Ask yourself, "Was it worth it?" Read further—God is giving you an acceptable way to live for the way in which you were born, but understand, sin is still sin. But you can be a homosexual who does not sin.

Don't let sin rule your body. After all, your body is bound to die, so don't obey its desires or let any part of it become a slave of evil. Give yourselves to God, as people who have been raised from death to life. Make every part of your body a slave that pleases God. Don't let sin keep ruling your lives. You are ruled by God's kindness and not by the Law.

Har'rell: Again, God wants us to let go of the things that are hindering us and keeping us in bondage, like drugs and sex. Can a man be a slave and still please God? No, he cannot. If you are a slave to your sin and desires, then that is your god.

Slaves Who Do What Pleases God

What does all this mean? Does it mean we are free to sin, because we are ruled by God's wonderful kindness and not by the Law? Certainly not! Don't you know that you are slaves of anyone you obey? You can be slaves of sin and die, or you can be obedient slaves of God and be acceptable to him. You used to be slaves of sin. But I thank God that with all your heart you obeyed the teaching you received from me. Now you are set free from sin and are slaves who please God.

Har'rell: In other words, yes, we are slaves to sin always because sin is our weakness. It is what causes us to fall short of God's glory every time, but we are set free from it. Do not fall back into something that God has delivered you from. When Lincoln freed the slaves, there were many who chose to remain slaves because they were afraid to step out on faith and start anew as being free from bondage, so they stayed with the wrong master. Are you going to choose the right master and free yourself from slavery of your mortal mind?

I am using these everyday examples, because in some ways you are still weak. You used to let the different parts of your body be slaves of your evil thoughts. But now you must make every part of your body serve God, so that you will belong completely to him.

Har'rell: A better example of this would be how you go to church every Sunday, smile and be prim and proper, leave church, and all the thoughts of how you are gonna tell so-and-so off later come full circle and you act on them. Now your body was in church praising and serving God, but guess what part of your body was not in service? that would be your mind. You allowed your mind to sin mentally before you physically did the act. It's also that way when we plan to fornicate or do drugs and commit other sins. It is nothing that just happened. Satan planted the thought, we let it simmer, then we planned on how to carry it out.

When you were slaves of sin, you didn't have to please God. But what good did you receive from the things you did? All you have to show for them is your shame, and they lead to death. Now you have been set free from sin, and you are God's slaves. This will make you holy and will lead you to eternal life. Sin pays off with death. But God's gift is eternal life given by Jesus Christ our Lord.

Romans 7 (Contemporary English Version) An Example from Marriage

My friends, you surely understand enough about law to know that laws only have power over people who are alive. For example, the Law says that a man's wife must remain his wife as long as he lives. But once her husband is dead, she is free to marry someone else. However, if she goes off with another man while her husband is still alive, she is said to be unfaithful.

That is how it is with you, my friends. You are now part of the body of Christ and are dead to the power of the Law. You are free to belong to Christ, who was raised to life so that we could serve God. When we thought only of ourselves, the Law made us have sinful desires. It made every part of our bodies into slaves who are doomed to die. But the Law no longer rules over us. We are like dead people, and it cannot have any power over us. Now we can serve God in a new way by obeying his Spirit and not in the old way by obeying the written Law.

Har'rell: I know you all are not going to like this, but before I go into it, let me give it to you this way first. First Corinthians 7:1–8 says the following:

Now for the matters you wrote about: It is good for a man not to marry. But since there is so much immorality, each man should have his own wife, and each woman her own husband. The husband should fulfill his marital duty to his wife, and likewise the wife to her husband. The wife's body does not belong to her alone but also to her husband. In the same way, the husband's body does not belong to him alone but also to his wife. Do not deprive each other except by mutual consent and for a time, so that you may devote yourselves to prayer. Then come together again so that Satan will not tempt you because of your lack of self-control. I say this as a concession, not as a command. I wish that all men were as I am. But each man has his own gift from God; one has this gift, another has that.

Now to the unmarried and the widows I say: It is good for them to stay unmarried, as I am. But if they cannot control themselves, they should marry, for it is better to marry than to burn with passion.

Har'rell: Right here is where I am about to go to battle with many people of the church. Who would you say God is speaking to? The unmarried are many of us who are widowed, never been married. Many homosexuals have never been married because we have been told by the church that we cannot. But here God tells us that it would be to our benefit to marry if we ca not control ourselves from fornication! Simple understanding, it is better to marry than to burn with passion or sin with consistent desire. He even said it was a concession (an offer of choice to do so) and not a command. Now God has also given the ability to marry over to the state. It has never been up to the church who should marry, just where you can marry, in the sanctuary or not. If not so, then why would you need to have a marriage license from the state for an ordained minister or state judge to perform the marriage? A state court judge can marry individuals, and they never have to enter the church. Again, the church has no say on who can and cannot marry. Do not get angry with me; get angry with the word you just read from God's Bible.

Religious beliefs have confused the Old and New Testament. God now says it is not good to sin when He offers so much to us who believe, worship, trust and have faith in Him. Now it is not only to those who are homosexual. this goes for those who are born with any imperfection that we may deem unworthy of leading a normal life. Mentally retarded citizens were once denied marriage because they were thought to be incapable of understanding marriage. But they understood love and the feeling of a soul mate that only a soul mate can bring. You may not believe it, but homosexuals have been able to find their soul mates, and many live healthy, holy, and acceptable lives unto God. They worship together, praise God just like you or I, and God uses them to be blessings to others. Then who are we to say God abhors them because of how they were born. He loves them enough to not want them to burn to their sins and simply marry and be acceptable.

I believe much promiscuity among the gay and lesbian community would end because of the comfort level to have one person in your life whom you do not have to hide behind closed doors. It's such behaviors that causes so many to feel they have to hide whom they love, and that hidden love becomes a strain on the relationship. And God still does not get the glory or the souls. God wants saved souls to build His kingdom up, not burdened and wounded spirits caused by man.

The Battle with Sin

Does this mean that the Law is sinful? Certainly not! But if it had not been for the Law, I would not have known what sin is really like. For example, I would not have known what it means to want something that belongs to someone else, unless the Law had told me not to do that. It was sin that used this command as a way of making me have all kinds of desires. But without the Law, sin is dead.

Before I knew about the Law, I was alive. But as soon as I heard that command, sin came to life, and I died. The very command that was supposed to bring life to me, instead brought death. Sin used this command to trick me, and because of it I died. Still, the Law and its commands are holy and correct and good.

Am I saying that something good caused my death? Certainly not! It was sin that killed me by using something good. Now we can see how terrible and evil sin really is. We know that the Law is spiritual. But I am merely a human, and I have been sold as a slave to sin. In fact, I don't understand why I act the way I do. I don't do what I know is right. I do the things I hate. Although I don't do what I know is right, I agree that the Law is good. So I am not the one doing these evil things. The sin that lives in me is what does them.

Har'rell: It is time for us to all take a step back, stop minding each other's business, and get the hell out of the way. It is not for us to judge anyone or decide whose sin God hates the most. He hates it all. But what we need to focus on is the sins that we are committing that He is watching you do daily. As soon as you hear some news of someone else, do you pick up the phone and talk about it? Gossiper. Do you take the extra change that the cashier gave you, knowing her draw will be short and may cost her, her job? Thief. Do you call in sick to work and are well just wanting to sleep in? Liar. Do you bat your eyes or make complimenting comments to your married co-worker? Coveter. I can go on and on and on, and guess what, eventually I will come to you. Now would you want me to make a public spectacle of your sins or shortcomings? Of course not.

I know that my selfish desires won't let me do anything that is good. Even when I want to do right, I cannot. Instead of doing what I know is right, I do wrong. And so, if I don't do what I know is right, I am no longer the one doing these evil things. The sin that lives in me is what does them.

The Law has shown me that something in me keeps me from doing what I know is right. With my whole heart I agree with the Law of God. But in every part of me I discover something fighting against my mind, and it makes me a prisoner of sin that controls everything I do. What a miserable person I am. Who will rescue me from this body that is doomed to die? Thank God! Jesus Christ will rescue me.

So with my mind I serve the Law of God, although my selfish desires make me serve the law of sin.

Har'rell: Clearly God understands our weakness to sin. However, we try to act like we don't sin anymore and have no interest in sinning, yet we do it in some form or fashion daily. Do you repent daily? I am not saying you should; I am just saying each and every day, we create a reason to repent. We are natural sinners who died to our sins, but the desire to sin does not. It's like abstaining from sex or drugs. You don't lose the desire to do it totally; you learn to refrain from the action, then eventually the desire will become weak and almost never surface.

Romans 8 (Contemporary English Version) Living by the Power of God's Spirit

If you belong to Christ Jesus, you won't be punished. The Holy Spirit will give you life that comes from Christ Jesus and will set you free from sin and death. The Law of Moses cannot do this, because our selfish desires make the Law weak. But God set you free when he sent his own Son to be like us sinners and to be a sacrifice for our sin. God used Christ's body to condemn sin. He did this, so that we would do what the Law commands by obeying the Spirit instead of our own desires. People who are ruled by their desires think only of themselves. Everyone who is ruled by the Holy Spirit thinks about spiritual things. If our minds are ruled by our desires, we will die. But if our minds are ruled by the Spirit, we will have life and peace. Our desires fight against God, because they do not and cannot obey God's laws. If we follow our desires, we cannot please God.

Har'rell: There was a saying, "If it feels good, do it." Funny, though—as good as sin feels during, it leaves you miserable and lost afterward. Again, God allows Paul to explain to us He will not stop you from sin. He will not save you from sin. He is not going to come in the midst of your sin to warn you that the consequences of your actions will lead to death or destruction. Renewing of the mind is important. If you think as you did before you were saved, then you will bring the desires that were unacceptable to God right along with you.

You are no longer ruled by your desires, but by God's Spirit, who lives in you. People who don't have the Spirit of Christ in them don't belong to him. But Christ lives in you. So you are alive because God has accepted you, even though your bodies must die because of your sins. Yet God raised Jesus to life! God's Spirit now lives in you, and he will raise you to life by his Spirit.

Har'rell: How fair is that? We have an amazing father, he gives us complete and total instructions on how to live God accepted lives, in spite of ourselves. We live to please God, not man. Every day we get up in the hopes of pleasing our boss or supervisor, pleasing our spouses, pleasing our parents. However, we do the minimum to please God. Yet it is His view of our lives that really matter. You can try to impress your boss for the new position; however, if you have not pleased God, He will not impart into the spirit of your boss to give you that promotion. Your promotion comes from God, not man. God uses man to give us earthly promotions.

My dear friends, we must not live to satisfy our desires. If you do, you will die. But you will live, if by the help of God's Spirit you say "No" to your desires. Only those people who are led by God's Spirit are his children. God's Spirit doesn't make us slaves who are afraid of him. Instead, we become his children and call him our Father. God's Spirit makes us sure that we are his children. His Spirit lets us know that together with Christ we will be given what God has promised.

We will also share in the glory of Christ, because we have suffered with him.

A Wonderful Future for God's People

I am sure that what we are suffering now cannot compare with the glory that will be shown to us. In fact, all creation is eagerly waiting for God to show who his children are. Meanwhile, creation is confused, but not because it wants to be confused. God made it this way in the hope that creation would be set free from decay and would share in the glorious freedom of his children. We know that all creation is still groaning and is in pain, like a woman about to give birth.

Har'rell: We say we are living in the last days, yet we live like we have time to get it right. Why are we confused to God? God allowed us to be confused. He allowed pastors and preachers to use His scripture for personal platform issues, knowing that we may walk away with doubt and confusion. God wants us to seek Him. So when in school and you have questions that were not answered in school, you read further in the text. God expects us to research Him, study Him, and live through Him, based on our knowledge of Him. Our world is in pain, war, floods, earthquakes, fires; all these things are signs that God is near. What may seem disastrous God sees as warning before destruction and rapture. Will you be caught up or left here?

The Spirit makes us sure about what we will be in the future. But now we groan silently, while we wait for God to show that we are his children. This means that our bodies will also be set free. And this hope is what saves us. But if we already have what we hope for, there is no need to keep on hoping. However, we hope for something we have not yet seen, and we patiently wait for it. In certain ways we are weak, but the Spirit is here to help us. For example, when we don't know what to pray for, the Spirit prays for us in ways that cannot be put into words. All of our thoughts are known to God. He can understand what is in the mind of the Spirit, as the Spirit prays for God's people. We know that God is always at work for the good of everyone who loves him. They are the ones God has chosen for his purpose, and he has always known who his chosen ones would be. He had decided to let them become like his own Son, so that his Son would be the first of many children. God then accepted the people he had already decided to choose, and he has shared his glory with them.

Har'rell: Let's break this down in simple terms. Everything we think about God knows we are thinking it. So why is it that when we do things behind one another's back, we feel like we got away with something? How foolish is the adulterer or liar or cheater or thief, when before you even committed the sin, God knew you had it premeditated, so when you find yourself in a *jam* afterward, your judge had already sentenced you while you were in the midst of your sin? You can choose to change your way of thinking to change your actions or wait for God to not choose you.

God's Love

What can we say about all this? If God is on our side, can anyone be against us? God did not keep back his own Son, but he gave him for us. If God did this, won't he freely give us everything

120

else? If God says his chosen ones are acceptable to him, can anyone bring charges against them? Or can anyone condemn them? No indeed! Christ died and was raised to life, and now he is at God's right side, speaking to him for us. Can anything separate us from the love of Christ? Can trouble, suffering, and hard times, or hunger and nakedness, or danger and death? It is exactly as the Scriptures say, "For you we face death all day long. We are like sheep on their way to be butchered."

Har'rell: No one knows the day nor the hour that God will return; all we know is that day is coming. However, each day someone dies and each day that we wake could be our last day. All God is asking is that with that in mind, live according to His law; don't get caught separating yourself from the Love of God. Get up each day like today could be you last, so live this day with love in your heart and faith that God will carry you through this day until it ends according to His will.

In everything we have won more than a victory because of Christ who loves us. I am sure that nothing can separate us from God's love— not life or death, not angels or spirits, not the present or the future, and not powers above or powers below. Nothing in all creation can separate us from God's love for us in Christ Jesus our Lord!

Romans 9
God's Choice of Israel

I am a follower of Christ, and the Holy Spirit is a witness to my conscience. So I tell the truth and I am not lying when I say my heart is broken and I am in great sorrow. I would gladly be placed under God's curse and be separated from Christ for the good of my own people. They are the descendants of Israel, and they are also God's chosen people. God showed them his glory. He made agreements with them and gave them his Law. The temple is theirs and so are the promises that God made to them. They have those famous ancestors, who were also the ancestors of Jesus Christ. I pray that God, who rules over all, will be praised forever! Amen. It cannot be said that God broke his promise. After all, not all of the people of Israel are the true people of God. In fact, when God made the promise to Abraham, he meant only Abraham's descendants by his son Isaac. God was talking only about Isaac when he promised Sarah, "At this time next year I will return, and you will already have a son."

Don't forget what happened to the twin sons of Isaac and Rebekah. Even before they were born or had done anything good or bad, the Lord told Rebekah that her older son would serve the younger one. The Lord said this to show that he makes his own choices and that it wasn't because of anything either of them had done. That's why the Scriptures say that the Lord liked Jacob more than Esau.

Are we saying that God is unfair? Certainly not! The Lord told Moses that he has pity and mercy on anyone he wants to. Everything then depends on God's mercy and not on what people want or do. In the Scriptures the Lord says to Pharaoh of Egypt, "I let you become Pharaoh, so that I could show you my power and be praised by all people on earth." Everything depends on what God decides to do, and he can either have pity on people or make them stubborn.

Har'rell: I wanted you to read this scripture all the way to the end because God gives us each ourselves in this stance even by saying *pharaoh*; that is like saying *pastor* here. What we want here on earth is irrelevant to God. We want society to be run a certain way. But have you ever stopped to think, How much would I be running up in heaven? How many things will I be in charge of? What courthouse can I go to in heaven to complain about homosexuals having rights or being married? Mercy, God's mercy, is what is sustaining us from what we really deserve from God. His wrath has been spared on you so many times, but if you look at the time we are living in, His wrath is coming forth. Pay attention when you know His mercy is upon you or when you have fallen from grace where mercy cannot be given. Discern within yourself the reasons it may or may not be upon you. "Have mercy on my soul"—this request is not always granted.

God's Anger and Mercy

Someone may ask, "How can God blame us, if he makes us behave in the way he wants us to?" But, my friend, I ask, "Who do you think you are to question God? Does the clay have the right to ask the potter why he shaped it the way he did? Doesn't a potter have the right to make a fancy bowl and a plain bowl out of the same lump of clay?"

Har'rell: Now let me make this clear: God is angry Yes, He is angry because His children are being persecuted and cast down and that is not His desire for us. He wants us to love one another and give each other the best of ourselves that we have to give. How dare we question His creations, His ways surpass that of our understanding, so how dare we simplify God to a mediocre level that

He would allow pastors, preachers, or even government officials to rule, control, or undermine His creations?- God wanted to show his anger and reveal his power against everyone who deserved to be destroyed. But instead, he patiently put up with them. He did this by showing how glorious he is when he has pity on the people he has chosen to share in his glory. Whether Jews or Gentiles, we are those chosen ones, just as the Lord says in the book of Hosea.

Har'rell: This one is easy. Interpreting the Holy Spirit, until now, has been a great challenge for me, but this is okay. He said He blesses us in front of you. When you close a door on us, he makes us your superior or He makes it so you have to depend on us. But because He has been patient with you and has not chastised you for your behavior toward others, you feel you are justified. Wrong, for every time you hurt someone else, imagine God taking away a blessing you never knew you had coming and giving it over to the person you just hurt. That's what God does; you just have not recognized what you are lacking from God. Each time you try to condemn anyone for their beliefs that are unlike yours or their orientation, which you do not self-righteously agree with, God takes a blessing from you and turns it over to them.

"Although they are not my people, I will make them my people. I will treat with love those nations that have never been loved." Once they were told, "You are not my people." But in that

122

very place they will be called children of the living God.

Har'rell: Once you told us because we were homosexual, God did not and will not accept us as saved, and we could not enter the kingdom of God. That's not what it says here. In the Old Testament, we were not His people because of the immoral acts as in Sodom and Gomorrah. They did not love God, respect God, nor believe in Him. However, we are the same people who have come to worship and adore Him in the New Testament. We have faith and He shows us favor. We do not revel in the history of Sodom and Gomorrah, nor do we pattern or conduct our lives to lead us to this type of behavior.

And this is what the prophet Isaiah said about the people of Israel, "The people of Israel are as many as the grains of sand along the beach. But only a few who are left will be saved. The Lord will be quick and sure to do on earth what he has warned he will do." Isaiah also said, "If the Lord All-Powerful had not spared some of our descendants, we would have been destroyed like the cities of Sodom and Gomorrah." Selah, Selah, Selah.

Israel and the Good News

What does all of this mean? It means that the Gentiles were not trying to be acceptable to God, but they found that he would accept them if they had faith. It also means that the people of Israel were not acceptable to God. And why not? It was because they were trying to be acceptable by obeying the Law instead of by having faith in God. The people of Israel fell over the stone that makes people stumble, just as God says in the Scriptures, "Look! I am placing in Zion a stone to make people stumble and fall. But those who have faith in that one will never be disappointed."

Har'rell: Yes, we have been made to stumble and fall in our lives, but God continues to sustain us and makes us prosperous, and it is all because of our faith in Him that although we stumble and even fall, we can back up and go to God all over again. All of us.

Romans 10 (Contemporary English Version)

Dear friends, my greatest wish and my prayer to God is for the people of Israel to be saved. I know they love God, but they don't understand what makes people acceptable to him. So they refuse to trust God, and they try to be acceptable by obeying the Law. But Christ makes the Law no longer necessary for those who become acceptable to God by faith.

Anyone Can Be Saved

Moses said that a person could become acceptable to God by obeying the Law. He did this when he wrote, "If you want to live, you must do all that the Law commands."

But people whose faith makes them acceptable to God will never ask, "Who will go up to heaven to bring Christ down?" Neither will they ask, "Who will go down into the world of the dead to raise him to life?"

All who are acceptable because of their faith simply say, "The message is as near as your mouth or your heart." And this is the same message we preach about faith. So you will be saved, if you honestly say, "Jesus is Lord," and if you believe with all your heart that God raised him from death. God will accept you and save you, if you truly believe this and tell it to others.

Har'rell: Anyone who says this and believes it in their heart are saved. Not because you took a right hand of fellowship; you don't lose your salvation because you did not complete new members class or miss two Sundays of church. Just believe it and be a witness to others that you are not only saved but that they would be happier and live a more acceptable life if they were saved as well.

The Scriptures say that no one who has faith will be disappointed, no matter if that person is a Jew or a Gentile. There is only one Lord, and he is generous to everyone who asks for his help. All who call out to the Lord will be saved.

Har'rell: I know this sermon will not reach everyone; however, ask yourself one question: Why would I not want and accept that everyone, even a crack head, thief, liar, fornicator, adulterer, or murderer, can be saved? To let the truth be told, I know a couple of former gangsters who are now pastors who have a body or two on their record, despite Moses's law "Thou shalt not kill." But the scripture says "All who call out the name of the Lord will be saved."

How can people have faith in the Lord and ask him to save them, if they have never heard about him? And how can they hear, unless someone tells them? And how can anyone tell them without being sent by the Lord? The Scriptures say it is a beautiful sight to see even the feet of someone coming to preach the good news. Yet not everyone has believed the message. For exam-

ple, the prophet Isaiah asked, "Lord, has anyone believed what we said?"

Har'rell: Now God used Paul all those years ago to set the tone for this sermon. I received this call to come from the entire book of Romans without ever having preached from the pulpit, ever evangelized, and ever being called to preach or pastor. God needed me, so I said yes. My pastor and his guest speakers all say the same thing: God can and will use whomever He chooses. I am honored that He not only used me for this He confirmed me in it.

No one can have faith without hearing the message about Christ. But am I saying that the people of Israel did not hear? No, I am not! The Scriptures say, "The message was told everywhere on earth. It was announced all over the world." Did the people of Israel understand or not? Moses answered this question when he told that the Lord had said, "I will make Israel jealous of people who are a nation of nobodies. I will make them angry at people who don't understand a thing." Isaiah was fearless enough to tell that the Lord had said, "I was found by people who were not looking for me. I appeared to the ones who were not asking about me." And Isaiah said about the people of Israel, "All day long the Lord has reached out to people who are stubborn and refuse to obey."

Har'rell: To some degree, I believe there is jealousy or envy among those who see God taking those whom we consider nobody in God's eye but are walking proud, driving nice, living well, working daily, and even gaining jobs during a recession. You have become angry because you do not understand. Try to understand that God loves us all the same. He is reaching out to you to love your neighbor, but you continue to be stubborn and refuse to obey.

Romans 11 (Contemporary English Version)
God Has Not Rejected His People

Am I saying that God has turned his back on his people? Certainly not! I am one of the people of Israel, and I myself am a descendant of Abraham from the tribe of Benjamin. God did not turn his back on his chosen people. Don't you remember reading in the Scriptures how Elijah complained to God about the people of Israel? He said, "Lord, they killed your prophets and destroyed your altars. I am the only one left, and now they want to kill me."

But the Lord told Elijah, "I still have seven thousand followers who have not worshiped Baal." It is the same way now. God was kind to the people of Israel, and so a few of them are still his followers. This happened because of God's undeserved kindness and not because of anything they have done. It could not have happened except for God's kindness. This means that only a chosen few of the people of Israel found what all of them were searching for. And the rest of them were stubborn, just as the Scriptures say, "God made them so stupid that their eyes are blind, and their ears are still deaf." Then David said, "Turn their meals into bait for a trap, so that they will stumble and be given what they deserve. Blindfold their eyes! Don't let them see. Bend their backs beneath a burden that will never be lifted."

Har'rell: This entire book has been designed by God in me from 2002 until 2009. It has been under His guidance and vigilance. Now it is released to you, this day, to open your eyes and make you not stupid. However, it is the stubborn man or self-righteous woman that God will allow you stay ignorant but responsible and accountable for what they now know but choose to ignore as God-given revelation. I personally am not concerned about those who do not believe that this is from God. He said He will make room for me and move those who come up against me. So I will not go toe-to-toe on any talk shows with those who disagree; I am not going to entertain those who want their television ratings to rise. If you choose to make this a media-driven issue, be my guest; I just won't be yours. Now those who wish to share in the joy that God is truly coming for a unified people and see this as a beginning to unify us, then I will be glad to sit next you and be interviewed. God has not rejected us, so I do not have to subject myself to man's rejection.

Gentiles Will Be Saved

Do I mean that the people of Israel fell, never to get up again? Certainly not! Their failure made it possible for the Gentiles to be saved, and this will make the people of Israel jealous. But if the rest of the world's people were helped so much by Israel's sin and loss, they will be helped even more by their full return.

Har'rell: Here is an example. We in the church of all sins make a sermon on homosexuality; however, we do not sermon on murder in our community or gangs in the schools killing our children. We do not sermon about the pedophiles chatting with and meeting our children off the Internet. We do not sermon about thieves and liars sitting next to us in a pew. Now because of it, God is aware that the church has become biased and prejudiced. So in front of you, He has and will continue to make you envy our blessings and envy our children, and here is the kicker . . . God says you envy our faith in Him. For it is you who do not understand how even after your efforts to persecute us and make us leave the church, our faith in God is all you see.

I am now speaking to you Gentiles, and as long as I am an apostle to you, I will take pride in my work. I hope in this way to make some of my own people jealous enough to be saved. When Israel rejected God, the rest of the people in the world were able to turn to him. So when God makes friends with Israel, it will be like bringing the dead back to life. If part of a batch of dough is made holy by being offered to God, then all of the dough is holy. If the roots of a tree are holy, the rest of the tree is holy too. You Gentiles are like branches of a wild olive tree that were made to be part of a cultivated olive tree. You have taken the place of some branches that were cut away from it. And because of this, you enjoy the blessings that come from being part of that culti-vated tree. But don't think you are better than the branches that were cut away. Just remember that you are not supporting the roots of that tree. Its roots are supporting you.

Har'rell: I love this. Think of your family tree. Each family member is a branch that can extend the tree with more branches or can be cut off by death or prison or drug addiction, but it does not make you better than that family member because you made well or are not on drugs; they are still a part of that tree. All God is saying is we were supposed to be born like everyone else, but we were born, like that of the wild, not cultivated. However, just because we were born different, we still receive the same blessings as anyone else who is from that tree.

Maybe you think those branches were cut away, so that you could be put in their place. That's true enough. But they were cut away because they did not have faith, and you are where you are because you do have faith. So don't be proud, but be afraid. If God cut away those natural branches, couldn't he do the same to you?

Har'rell: Faith is powerful. It is the tie that binds us together. Without it, we are cut away from one another. Now for those of you who are homosexual who are reading this, this is not a time for you to gloat or say, "Yeah, I knew it would come out sooner or later." Stay humble for God is still your judge.

Now you see both how kind and how hard God can be. He was hard on those who fell, but he was kind to you. And he will keep on being kind to you, if you keep on trusting in his kind-ness. Otherwise, you will be cut away too.

If those other branches will start having faith, they will be made a part of that tree again. God has the power to put them back. After all, it wasn't natural for branches to be cut from a wild olive tree and to be made part of a cultivated olive tree. So it is much more likely that God will join the natural branches back to the cultivated olive tree.

Har'rell: Whew! This is deep, God! Those who have fallen short of God's glory can come back to Him. Now I like the part that says it wasn't natural for branches to be cut from a wild olive tree and be made a part of a cultivated olive tree. Now let's go back to chapter one, where the wives and husbands decided to have unnatural relations with the same sex. God says here even they will be joined more than likely through their faith and deliverance back to the cultivated olive tree. Now regarding to the homosexual, it was not common in our world for God to place us equally in marriage to create extended branches, but He has done so. For those who have faith in Him and seek to live an acceptable life unto God, He grants you favor. I have a friend who recently called me to inform me that he was approved to adopt two toddler-stage boys, ages one and two. He is a homosexual, saved, a good man. He has a wonderful career and does not drink nor smoke. He is developing his tree and extending the branches. God has already blessed him. There is nothing we can say or do whether we agree or not.

The People of Israel Will Be Brought Back

My friends, I don't want you Gentiles to be too proud of yourselves. So I will explain the mystery of what has happened to the people of Israel. Some of them have become stubborn, and they will stay like that until the complete number of you Gentiles has come in. In this way all of Israel will be saved, as the Scriptures say.

Har'rell: Time and matters of times past seem to be repeating themselves. We are many years from this time; however, God has to reveal it to us once again in our time and set this up for a time such as this.

This is a time where we have become a society of technical and scientific wonders. We have the unsaved media that influences our way of thinking, our belief of what is going on around us, and whom we should like and dislike. God wants us to be on one accord in Him.

"From Zion someone will come to rescue us. Then Jacob's descendants will stop being evil. This is what the Lord has promised to do when he forgives their sins." The people of Israel are treated as God's enemies, so that the good news can come to you Gentiles. But they are still the chosen ones, and God loves them because of their famous ancestors. God doesn't take back the gifts he has given or forget about the people he has chosen. At one time you Gentiles rejected God. But now Israel has rejected God, and you have been shown mercy. And because of the mercy shown to you, they will also be shown mercy. All people have disobeyed God, and that's why he treats them as prisoners. But he does this, so that he can have mercy on all of them.

Har'rell: Yes, at one time, those who were cast down and set apart like those of Sodom and Gomorrah did not receive God as their God, and they rejected God. But now the same Gentiles have faith and show reverence to God, and it pleases Him, whether you like it or not. He is pleased and shows mercy upon them. Why won't we let God be God and stop trying to keep Him defined to fit who we want Him to be and how we want Him to judge others?

Who can measure the wealth and wisdom and knowledge of God? Who can understand his decisions or explain what he does? Has anyone known the thoughts of the Lord or given him advice? Has anyone loaned something to the Lord that must be repaid?" Everything comes from the Lord. All things were made because of him and will return to him. Praise the Lord forever! Amen.

Har'rell: I am not saying all these years of preaching and teaching you who deliver the word on a regular basis have been wrong. God is just saying you have made Him fit into a box of religious beliefs that are lower than His ways and understanding. He says that you have become personal from the pulpit. He has accepted your numerous sermons on tithing when the bills and finances have been misappropriated. He has pardoned your displays of wealth and riches among those in your congregation who suffer and struggle weekly even to make it to service. He has even allowed you back into the pulpit after your own indiscretions, given you a word for His people, knowing the things you have done behind closed doors. Understand, pastors and preachers, as long as there is a God, then you to have to bow down and receive Him as others have to receive Him through you. God says that He is bringing all of you who preach the gospel in 2010 to a higher level of understanding. When you read His Word this year and years to come, rhema will fall each time you try to invoke yourself. Your tongues He will control and keep you on His path for His people. Pastors and preachers, I have not read the book of Jeremiah, and I can admit that; however, God says you need to go back and read thoroughly the book of Jeremiah. Then you will understand what He means by a new level of understanding in Him. Thus saith the Lord.

Romans 12 (Contemporary English Version) Christ Brings New Life

Dear friends, God is good. So I beg you to offer your bodies to him as a living sacrifice, pure and pleasing. That's the most sensible way to serve God. Don't be like the people of this world, but let God change the way you think. Then you will know how to do everything that is good and pleasing to him. I realize how kind God has been to me, and so I tell each of you not to think you are better than you really are. Use good sense and measure yourself by the amount of faith that God has given you. A body is made up of many parts, and each of them has its own use. That's how it is with us. There are many of us, but we each are part of the body of Christ, as well as part of one another. God has also given each of us different gifts to use. If we can prophesy, we should do it according to the amount of faith we have. If we can serve others, we should serve. If we can teach, we should teach. If we can encourage others, we should encourage them. If we can give, we should be generous. If we are leaders, we should do our best. If we are good to others, we should do it cheerfully.

Har'rell: I love the fact that as I read then give revelation, God gives me revelation and confirmation. God raised me up with the natural ability to blend words together and make them show you vivid, true images even if it is make-believe. However, he has also used my writing skills to solve tremendous issues in others' lives, seal deals, write grant proposals and business plans, start others in business, and express love. As He calls me to use my talents, I immediately do what He has commissioned me to do. So I was not surprised, just taken back, when God requested this of me. I sought preacher friends, colleagues, and family about this, and all said it was time for this, and they received God in it. I absolutely love people, all people. I don't know why; I just do. I hate to see anyone hurting, and I have given and will continue to give to those less fortunate. I have taught my son to give not just money but of himself. That is the first step in allowing God to make room for your gifts: start by serving others . . .

Rules for Christian Living

Be sincere in your love for others. Hate everything that is evil and hold tight to everything that is good. Love each other as brothers and sisters and honor others more than you do yourself. Never give up. Eagerly follow the Holy Spirit and serve the Lord. Let your hope make you glad. Be patient in times of trouble and never stop praying. Take care of God's needy people, and welcome strangers into your home.

Har'rell: I am guilty of this; I admit it. I have taken in strangers—my son is a witness—even fell in love with a couple of them. However, I always knew that God sent them, so I opened my doors and my heart. It was challenging; at times, I wondered if I bit off more than I can chew. They made sure my good deed did not go unpunished. However, once I have done for God what He needed me to do, in His

own way, He removed them. I know we are living in a time when you have to be safe and protect your home and family. But please use discernment, for you never know how God can use that individual in your life and you in theirs.

Ask God to bless everyone who mistreats you. Ask him to bless them and not to curse them. When others are happy, be happy with them, and when they are sad, be sad. Be friendly with everyone. Don't be proud and feel that you are smarter than others. Make friends with ordinary people. Don't mistreat someone who has mistreated you. But try to earn the respect of others, and do your best to live at peace with everyone. Dear friends, don't try to get even. Let God take revenge. In the Scriptures the Lord says, "I am the one to take revenge and pay them back." The Scriptures also say, "If your enemies are hungry, give them something to eat. And if they are thirsty, give them something to drink. This will be the same as piling burning coals on their heads." Don't let evil defeat you, but defeat evil with good.

Har'rell: Some of the very ones I have helped mistreated me, disrespected me in my own home, and even stole from me. I do not get even or try to ruin their lives. I just notice how they prosper. They never seem to be totally happy, and I continue to seek and serve God. My joy comes from the fact of knowing that whenever they left, they left better than they came. I have nothing to be angry about. And the pain from hurt by man subsides eventually.

Romans 13 (Contemporary English Version)
Obey Rulers

Obey the rulers who have authority over you. Only God can give authority to anyone, and he puts these rulers in their places of power. People who oppose the authorities are opposing what God has done, and they will be punished. Rulers are a threat to evil people, not to good people. There is no need to be afraid of the authorities. Just do right, and they will praise you for it. After all, they are God's servants, and it is their duty to help you.

Har'rell: Even those in government, including the president, are serving God. Without God, there would have been no Obama. However, we knew it was time to allow God to intervene on our country and give us a ruler who has His favor and will do His will. Now this may not be how we see it, but Obama belongs to God, and God does not care how you see it. He just expects everyone—Republican, Democrat, Independent, whatever worldly class you have assumed—to know He has made him ruler over this nation and governor of the world. He has given him the ability, and he, along with this wife, has the gift to unify a people.

If you do something wrong, you ought to be afraid, because these rulers have the right to punish you. They are God's servants who punish criminals to show how angry God is. But you should obey the rulers because you know it is the right thing to do, and not just because of God's anger.

Har'rell: We tend to forget that even police officers have special gifts that allow them to embrace their authority and place a measure of concern when they are present. Their uniforms command authority; they can punish us like children and lock us in a room. It angers God when we disobey the laws of the land.

You must also pay your taxes. The authorities are God's servants, and it is their duty to take care of these matters. Pay all that you owe, whether it is taxes and fees or respect and honor.

Har'rell: In other words, it is taxpayers' money that pays the authority that protects us and keeps us safer than if they did not exist. Be diligent in paying what you owe in taxes for it does not belong to you alone.

Love

Let love be your only debt! If you love others, you have done all that the Law demands. In the Law there are many commands, such as, "Be faithful in marriage. Do not murder. Do not steal. Do not want what belongs to others." But all of these are summed up in the command that says, "Love others as much as you love yourself." No one who loves others will harm them. So love is all that the Law demands.

Har'rell: We who love the Lord must be careful that our love is not selfish and only given to God. At that point, you are placing yourself in an awkward position with God. He did not command us to only love Him. He has commanded, instructed, and shown authority in His command to love one another as yourself. Now if you are batting with how to love yourself, you may find that it is the source of failed relationships or troubled friendships. Begin to treat yourself with the same respect, kindness, and care that you would someone you would pursue for love. Then watch how the outpour of love you give to yourself spills over to your treatment of others. God does not hate you if you do not love all His children; it just holds up your blessings that He has in store for you. I have been hurt before by many people who said they loved me. Even though they hurt me and scandalized my name, when God sent them back to me, I did not turn my back on them; I helped them. I forgave them for what they did to me when they did it. That is love in spite of . . .

The Day When Christ Returns

You know what sort of times we live in, and so you should live properly. It is time to wake up. You know that the day when we will be saved is nearer now than when we first put our faith in the Lord. Night is almost over, and day will soon appear. We must stop behaving as people do in the dark and be ready to live in the light. So behave properly, as people do in the day. Don't go to wild parties or get drunk or be vulgar or indecent. Don't quarrel or be jealous. Let the Lord Jesus Christ be as near to you as the clothes you wear. Then you won't try to satisfy your selfish desires.

Har'rell: Many of us believers take lightly the things we do that God wants us to pull away from, because it is not healthy for our spiritual growth. Each year that we see, God makes the days shorter, and the months seem to over-lap; they come in so fast. But that is just God showing us that the time is drawing near, and as He is returning, we are not in preparation. Look at this as it was a surprise party for God. You do not know what time He is coming; you just know He is. Like a surprise party where the guests prepare for the honored individual, God is showing us that we must prepare for His coming as well. Speak life into each other, stop condemning those who may still need time to learn and grow at their own pace, and stop finding more solace in the nightclubs and bars than you do in Christ. Practice talking through our anger instead of arguing without any solutions. Our flesh has a way of controlling us. We satisfy it with drugs, sex, partying, and selfish living. God is not only displeased; He is jealous.

Romans 14
Don't Criticize Others

Welcome all the Lord's followers, even those whose faith is weak. Don't criticize them for having beliefs that are different from yours. Some think it is all right to eat anything, while those whose faith is weak will eat only vegetables. But you should not criticize others for eating or for not eating. After all, God welcomes everyone. What right do you have to criticize someone else's servants? Only their Lord can decide if they are doing right, and the Lord will make sure that they do right.

Some of the Lord's followers think one day is more important than another. Others think all days are the same. But each of you should make up your own mind. Any followers who count one day more important than another day do it to honor their Lord. And any followers who eat meat give thanks to God, just like the ones who don't eat meat.

Whether we live or die, it must be for God, rather than for ourselves. Whether we live or die, it must be for the Lord. Alive or dead, we still belong to the Lord. This is because Christ died and rose to life, so that he would be the Lord of the dead and of the living. Why do you criticize other followers of the Lord? Why do you look down on them? The day is coming when God will judge all of us. In the Scriptures God says.

Har'rell: I like this chapter because it calls out so many of us who perpetrate our Christianity then when we are not in church or Bible study, we display our disdain for one another. We talk about our co-workers and what they don't have. We pass judgment as though we are authorities on humanism. God did not assign us to judge others for Him, nor does He make judgments on us based on what you believe. Clean your house, keep it in order, and don't worry about the next man's house unless you are going to bless it. Watch what you say about your neighbor; watch how you treat your neighbor because God is watching you.

"I swear by my very life that everyone will kneel down and praise my name!" And so, each of us must give an account to God for what we do.

Don't Cause Problems for Others

We must stop judging others. We must also make up our minds not to upset anyone's faith. The Lord Jesus has made it clear to me that God considers all foods fit to eat. But if you think some foods are unfit to eat, then for you they are not fit.

Har'rell: This goes back to what I said about different religions. We may not believe as Baptist that God has a purgatory in which Catholics believe. God is saying that food in which they were taught under was tailor-made for them, and that is why they are Catholic and not Baptist. "No one comes to the Father but by me." Jesus let us know this, so whether or not your religion teaches you something different from others, respect their beliefs, cling to your own, and allow God to meet you where you are, not where they are.

If you are hurting others by the foods you eat, you are not guided by love. Don't let your appetite destroy someone Christ died for. Don't let your right to eat bring shame to Christ. God's kingdom isn't about eating and drinking. It is about pleasing God, about living in peace, and about true happiness. All this comes from the Holy Spirit. If you serve Christ in this way, you will please God and be respected by people. We should try to live at peace and help each other have a strong faith. Don't let your appetite destroy what God has done. All foods are fit to eat, but it is wrong to cause problems for others by what you eat. It is best not to eat meat or drink wine or do anything else that causes problems for other followers of the Lord. What you believe about these things should be kept between you and God. You are fortunate, if your actions don't make you have doubts. But if you do have doubts about what you eat, you are going against your beliefs. And you know that is wrong, because anything you do against your beliefs is sin.

Har'rell: Let's just say Sister Sadie goes to church every Sunday, Bible study on Wednesday, and revivals. She has a tremendous knowledge of who God is in her life. However, she has children and a husband who will only watch thirty minutes of a televangelist. She constantly tells them that they are not getting all of what God wants them to know. She acts as though they will not know God until they come to church with her. As much as I love Sadie for her reverence to God, I have to say to Sadie, "You are wrong." God will meet us where we are, even if it is in your bed while watching Joyce Meyer. God will meet you there. So do not think what you have is greater and you have the key that unlocks all that God has. Sadie can ultimately anger God while He is trying to raise up someone with other food. Just continue to eat yours. If a man will not eat your food, then maybe he is on a different diet.

Romans 15 (Contemporary English Version) Please Others and Not Yourself

If our faith is strong, we should be patient with the Lord's followers whose faith is weak. We should try to please them instead of ourselves. We should think of their good and try to help them by doing what pleases them. Even Christ did not try to please himself. But as the Scriptures say, "The people who insulted you also insulted me." And the Scriptures were written to teach and encourage us by giving us hope. God is the one who makes us patient and cheerful. I pray that he will help you live at peace with each other, as you follow Christ. Then all of you together will praise God, the Father of our Lord Jesus Christ.

Har'rell: When I get up in the morning, I do not say "Lord, this is the day that I have made. Let me be glad and rejoice in it," because it was not I who made the next day, nor do I construct the way it will operate. I can plan to, but God has that control. What I do say is, "Lord make me a blessing to others," because I understand that the principles of my faith, my purpose, and my beliefs in Him rest on my making others feel fulfilled. Pleasing others does not mean doing what others want you to do. It means helping those whom God sends, telling someone "I love you, I am praying for you" and really doing it and meaning it. We can please each other just by yielding to what the other may be going through.

The Good News Is for Jews and Gentiles

Honor God by accepting each other, as Christ has accepted you. I tell you that Christ came as a servant of the Jews to show that God has kept the promises he made to their famous ancestors. Christ also came, so that the Gentiles would praise God for being kind to them. It is just as the Scriptures say, "I will tell the nations about you, and I will sing praises to your name." The Scriptures also say to the Gentiles, "Come and celebrate with God's people." Again the Scriptures say, "Praise the Lord, all you Gentiles. All you nations, come and worship him." Isaiah says, "Someone from David's family will come to power. He will rule the nations, and they will put their hope in him." I pray that God, who gives hope, will bless you with complete happiness and peace because of your faith. And may the power of the Holy Spirit fill you with hope.

Har'rell: Regarding all our personal beliefs, our dislikes for other races, sexual orientations, and anything we do not understand, God says you love Him, yet His ways surpass any level of understanding we can have. But we cannot love one another. However, this is where we are being called to, this is the level of Christ we are. God does not care what you personally believe about the next person's life or lifestyle. What you believe and have believed about God is far from where God is and His views. If you truly want to honor God, accept each other for whom God created. He created the liar, the beggar, the thief, the drunkard, and those whom you may not agree with the way they live. God wants us to be happy on earth and live in harmony. If we think that God ordained these wars, we have another thought coming. He said there will be rumors of war. Meaning of course we can bring war to the table, but God wants us to fight against the enemy that we cannot see for the God we cannot see. If we love other countries instead of fighting against them, then we would be more in line with the divine will of God for our life.

Paul's Work as a Missionary

My friends, I am sure that you are very good and that you have all the knowledge you need to teach each other. But I have spoken to you plainly and have tried to remind you of some things. God was so kind to me! He chose me to be a servant of Christ Jesus for the Gentiles and to do the work of a priest in the service of his good news. God did this so that the Holy Spirit could make the Gentiles into a holy offering, pleasing to him.

Because of Christ Jesus, I can take pride in my service for God. In fact, all I will talk about is how Christ let me speak and work, so that the Gentiles would obey him. Indeed, I will tell how Christ worked miracles and wonders by the power of the Holy Spirit. I have preached the good news about him all the way from Jerusalem to Illyricum. But I have always tried to preach where people have never heard about Christ. I am like a builder who doesn't build on anyone else's foundation. It is just as the Scriptures say, "All who haven't been told about him will see him and those who haven't heard about him will understand."

Har'rell: God has provided us with this message not just for those who know God. That is why the beginning of this book had familiar words that people whom we call worldly would use. In that, they are also able to be reached. Then He brought forth revelation. That is the awesomeness of our God. He wants everyone. It is our mission as believers to go out and be missionaries for God. Instead of looking down on others or toward them, pastors preach each week to someone who does not know and has never heard about what God can do in their life. For those who do not enter into the temple or church or mosque or synagogue, it is us who do enter into these places of worship that must learn how to continue the worship experience with others. God gives us many ways to go out and give what we have been given. There are music and sermon CDs and DVDs, televangelists that are on fire! God has already laid the foundation for us. Now He expects us to be builders of His kingdom, not tear it down with our natural ways but our supernatural power within. God said, "Unleash it and go out to serve Me."

Paul's Plan to Visit Rome

My work has always kept me from coming to see you. Now there is nothing left for me to do in this part of the world, and for years I have wanted to visit you. So I plan to stop off on my way to Spain. Then after a short, but refreshing, visit with you, I hope you will quickly send me on.

I am now on my way to Jerusalem to deliver the money that the Lord's followers in Macedonia and Achaia collected for God's needy people. This is something they really wanted to do. But sharing their money with the Jews was also like paying back a debt, because the Jews had already shared their spiritual blessings with the Gentiles. After I have safely delivered this money, I will visit you and then go on to Spain. And when I do arrive in Rome, I know it will be with the full blessings of Christ.

My friends, by the power of the Lord Jesus Christ and by the love that comes from the Holy Spirit, I beg you to pray sincerely with me and for me. Pray that God will protect me from the unbelievers in Judea, and that his people in Jerusalem will be pleased with what I am doing. Ask God to let me come to you and have a pleasant and refreshing visit. I pray that God, who gives peace, will be with all of you. Amen.

Har'rell: Do you hear how excited Paul was to make this journey, to deliver to a people a word to save their lives? Imagine now just as the cycle and circle of life brings us back to this very place. Paul's words resonate no differently than if He were speaking to us in our time, in the flesh. God knew that many gen-

erations would receive His word, but He also knew that because of generational curses, we are doomed to repeat the same things just during a different time. God is drawing closer, you Joshua children of God! (If you were under the age of twenty-five when the year 2000 came in, this is your time.) God has equipped you all with new visions, ideas that have never been done before. He did not invoke a recession by happenstance; He is taking from the greedy, the selfish, the wicked, and those in between riches, wealth, health, and security, bringing them to the level of worry and poverty, which they have caused so many of His people. And He is storing their homes, their buildings, and their offices and turning it over to a new realm of God. Their will be businesses again, but they must know that any business must honor God. For the seeds sown to make it happen came from nowhere else. So now all you who have your own business or want your own business, if you do not recognize that by other than by God, you would not have been! God said your business will no longer prosper in this time without acknowledging Him. God is calling us to a place we have never been because we have never been this close to His coming. Even in the midst of war and famine, tsunamis, hurricanes, and floods that wipe out cities, I cannot help but see the hand of God trying to get our attention through His works that no matter how technologically sound we think we are, we cannot stop God's power of nature. I laugh sometimes when we spend millions to billions trying to defy God's weather or predict what the next day is going to be like. Paul and so many others whom God has given revelation to are taken too lightly by us. What would we do if God just suddenly stops giving us revelation? We would be lost, a world with no rules and no laws. And most of us, if not all of us, would be doomed to not enter into the kingdom realm of God when we leave this earth. Practice peace. As a matter of fact, I think I am going to come out with a line of T-shirts that simply says "Practice peace." In order for us to get to that place, we must each individually, daily, bring the spirit of peace into our hearts, homes, jobs, and in our daily contact with others.

Romans 16 (Contemporary English Version) Personal Greetings

I have good things to say about Phoebe, who is a leader in the church at Cenchreae. Welcome her in a way that is proper for someone who has faith in the Lord and is one of God's own people. Help her in any way you can. After all, she has proved to be a respected leader for many others, including me.

Give my greetings to Priscilla and Aquila, they have not only served Christ Jesus together with me, but they have even risked their lives for me. I am grateful for them and so are all the Gentile churches. Greet the church that meets in their home. Greet my dear friend Epaenetus, who was the first person in Asia to have faith in Christ. Greet Mary, who has worked so hard for you. Greet my relatives Andronicus and Junias, who were in jail with me. They are highly respected by the apostles and were followers of Christ before I was. Greet Ampliatus, my dear friend whose faith is in the Lord. Greet Urbanus, who serves Christ along with us. Greet my dear friend Stachys. Greet Apelles, a faithful servant of Christ. Greet Aristobulus and his family. Greet Herodion, who is a relative of mine. Greet Narcissus and the others in his family, who have faith in the Lord. Greet Tryphaena and Tryphosa, who work hard for the Lord. Greet my dear friend Persis. She also works hard for the Lord. Greet Rufus, that special servant of the Lord, and greet his mother, who has been like a mother to me. Greet Asyncritus, Phlegon, Hermes, Patrobas, and Hermas, as well as our friends who are with them. Greet Philologus, Julia, Nereus and his sister, and Olympas, and all of God's people who are with them. Be sure to give each other a warm greeting.

Har'rell: Wow! Paul even took the time to acknowledge those who are just common, everyday people. Not our superheroes of the bible who performed wonders and miracles. No, just those who worked for the Lord. Are you receiving this? Even Paul knew that everyone was important to the kingdom of God. Now their names are written in this holy text for eternity. I want to be remembered by God for my works for Him strengthening His kingdom. Not for my cocaine addiction, not for my crack usage, not for my drinking and stirring up mess, not for my wasting years of my life, but for my works. What have you done to increase the kingdom? Do you understand that we must?

All of Christ's Churches Greet You

My friends, I beg you to watch out for anyone who causes trouble and divides the church by refusing to do what all of you were taught. Stay away from them! They want to serve themselves and not Christ the Lord. Their flattery and fancy talk fool people who don't know any better. I am glad that everyone knows how well you obey the Lord. But still, I want you to understand what is good and not have anything to do with evil. Then God, who gives peace, will soon crush Satan under your feet. I pray that our Lord Jesus will be kind to you.

Har'rell: For those of you who will want to disagree with this word from the Lord, those who will protest its very being, as much as I would like to entertain your controversy, God said that I cannot. God has given me revelation, and just like you cannot challenge Him directly, you cannot challenge Him indirectly by challenging me. I am glad He ended it this way for me. Being chosen to do this was difficult to accept, but when I look over my life, at all the people whom God has led me to help, the love that I have for all people of any race, I could not deny being chosen. You cannot express or request love if you do not give it yourself.

Timothy, who works with me, sends his greetings, and so do my relatives, Lucius, Jason, and Sosipater. I, Tertius, also send my greetings. I am a follower of the Lord, and I wrote this letter. Gaius welcomes me and the whole church into his home, and he sends his greetings. Erastus, the city treasurer, and our dear friend Quartus send their greetings too.

Paul's Closing Prayer

Praise God! He can make you strong by means of my good news, which is the message about Jesus Christ. For ages and ages this message was kept secret, but now at last it has been told. The eternal God commanded his prophets to write about the good news, so that all nations would obey and have faith. And now, because of Jesus Christ, we can praise the only wise God forever! Amen.

HAR'RELL'S
Closing Prayer

Dear Lord, I pray this day and unto the day you return to reclaim us that your words do not come back void, that your children understand that they are not their own, that they do belong to you. That the laws in which you have commanded us we begin to enforce in our daily lives. Lord, impart in all men's hearts that you do exist, that you do have control over our days. I pray that men shall live and not die to the things that make us weak. Dear Lord, you are our source, our strength, and our redeemer. We bow before you in your magnificence! Amen.

CPSIA information can be obtained
at www.ICGtesting.com
Printed in the USA
LVHW070625231118
597737LV00006B/57/P